TAKE ME

ALSO BY CD REISS

THE DILUSTRO ARRANGEMENT

An epic mafia romance trilogy.

Some girls dream of marrying a prince, but I never imagined I'd be sold to a king.

Mafia Bride | Mafia King | Mafia Queen

THE GAMES DUET

Adam Steinbeck will give his wife a divorce on one condition. She join him in a remote cabin for 30 days, submitting to his sexual dominance.

Marriage Games | Separation Games

THE EDGE SERIES

Rough. Edgy. Sexy enough to melt in your hands.

Rough Edge | On The Edge | Broken Edge | Over the Edge

THE SUBMISSION SERIES

Monica insists she's not submissive. Jonathan Drazen is going to prove otherwise, but he might fall in love doing it.

One Night With Him | One Year With Him | One Life With Him

TAKE ME

MANHATTAN MAFIA - BOOK ONE

CD REISS

For everyone who slowed to a standstill in the first year of the pandemic. I was with you.

CHAPTER 1

SARAH

NEW YORK CITY

IT'S MY WEDDING DAY, AND I CAN'T BREATHE.

With one hand on either side of the window frame, I look down over the city and across the East River, where the sun is rising, gritting my teeth against the discomfort in my ribs. It's still dark enough outside to reflect my face's pained contortions.

Grandma Marta can see she's hurting me, but she pulls the strings tighter anyway.

Last night, at the dinner with the Agostis, I served the food but ate nothing, and they commented on what a good wife I'd make for Sergio.

I've spent my whole life getting ready for this day. Avoiding food to fit into this corset was nothing.

"One more," Grandma says. "Make the Colonia proud."

I empty my lungs and nod.

She pulls. "Good!"

When the strings are tied off and the back zipped, I stand straight and look at myself in the mirror. The corset is hidden under a more modest white shell that zips over the lacing. Tonight, after the reception, Sergio will see the corset when he removes the outside. Then he'll remove me from my childhood and place me inside the society of women.

"So, then," Grandma says. "You're going to have a husband."

She's suspicious of this match, and though she knows it's not my fault or my choice, she can't hide her disapproval from me.

"It's an important day for us, Grandma. All of us. It's the first time a Colonia has—"

"No." She holds out her hand to stop me from saying another word. "It's not the first time one of us has married outside Precious Blood. No. Don't fool yourself. It's the first time it's been done for politics. For territory. For money."

"Daddy knows what he's doing."

She shouldn't be questioning my father. He's been running the Colonia for as long as I can remember. We live all over the city in a web of silent connections. Daddy is the king of us all. He keeps us safe, manages disputes, quietly rules over our little slice of New York from the secret closed church of Precious Blood.

"Let's hope so."

Grandma is my mother's mother, and we're all descended from the first Colonia. When Mommy died, Daddy got us a bigger apartment and brought her up to live with us. Someone had to take care of Massimo and me—so she's invested in us and afraid I'll be less than I was raised to be.

"I don't like giving you up to strangers," she adds.

"I'm scared," I say, putting my hand on her shoulder. My face tingles, and my nose tickles. I'm going to cry again.

She slides me into an embrace too careful to mess up my hair. "The Agosti family has the same values as we do. Think of it as us bringing them in."

I nod against her. She's said it a million times, and she's still right, but I'm still terrified of entering this new world. "I know."

"Don't cry." Grandma pushes me away, keeping her hands on my shoulders as if our eyes are on the same level. "You are Sarah Colonia, and you are proud. You will not arrive at Precious Blood late with ruined makeup."

"I won't."

She takes me by the chin. "You will be beautiful. You will be pristine. And you will be given into marriage today."

"I will. Thank you." My tears have stopped. I do feel better.

Her hand drops. "We need to talk about tonight, peanut."

"I know how to give him what he wants." I can't look at her while thinking about the details of the act itself. "I know it's going to hurt."

Denise beat Grandma to it—talking about sex in every detail since she got married four years ago. But Grandma never wants to hear about my best friend, that no-good whore.

"You just stay still." She strokes back my hair. "It'll be over soon enough."

The door slaps open, and we both spin around to my younger brother, Massimo, storming in.

3

"Goody." His nickname for me is short for "goody two shoes" and comes from all the times I've stopped him from doing something stupid. Like drinking from the liquor cabinet or smoking a cigar butt Daddy left in the ashtray. He's already in his tux, but his top two shirt buttons are open. "What's taking so long?"

"Put your tie on," Grandma demands.

He ignores her. Massimo does what he wants, the way he wants, no more or less. The tie will probably stay in his pocket until the last minute.

"Such a hurry to get to church." Slowly, I put my satin gloves into the little purse that matches my dress. "You haven't seen the inside of it in years."

"Because it's all bullshit and it's boring."

"Don't talk like that." Grandma gathers my shawl and scans the room to make sure we have everything. We do. But she's tormenting Massimo as much as I am because he's a man and has all the freedom in the world. All we can do is delay.

"Don't rush me on *my* day just because you want *your* prize." In the mirror, I check my lashes, my hair, the lay of my dress. "Now, what else am I forgetting?"

"You're forgetting to move it like you mean it." He adjusts his cuffs in the mirror. "You're not getting any younger."

He has a point. I'm twenty-one.

"And you need to be a little older." I jab his side with a bent finger. "Before you start bossing people around."

He laughs and pulls me to him with one arm, side to side.

4

I stand next to him, framing us in the reflection. "Spoiled little prince."

"King-in-training as of today." He's been waiting for me to get married so he can move up in the family—even above any husband I might take.

"As of Armistice Night," I tease. "You're not officially the successor until then."

Last year, on the night the most important families of our world gathered in truce, my father brought me to Armistice Night. I was the talk of the evening with my white dress and red sash, broadcasting that I was a virgin available for a marriage to unite kingdoms. More than that though, I was a walking notice that the Colonia was ready to come up from the underground. I stood behind my father's chair as men approached my father to ask about my availability and pitch their sons and grandsons.

"Today is your day, Goody."

"So it is, Emo." I take his arm. "So it is."

CHAPTER 2

SARAH

THE AUTUMN SUN'S FIRST RAYS SPILL FROM THE SKY AND RUSH between the buildings, blushing the white silk of my dress a sweet, shimmering pink. It was dark when I woke, cool blue light rendering the world outside my window in smudges and shadow, but now the sunrise is a riot of color in the slit of sky between the buildings of First Avenue—a gift to Manhattan's early-morningers. The security guards with their thick-fingered gloves and the night nannies smelling of diapers, the bagel makers and coffee grinders, they trudge up, headfirst, from the subway in a daily rite where the first sight of their day is the only thing we share—the most magnificent sky I've ever seen.

I can't help feeling like the intense, singular beauty of the heavens on my wedding day is a good sign and that I too am being born into the warm core of a city populated with people who have no idea I exist.

The Colonia exists astride the world and outside it. We are born, baptized, and married without public record. We die without word to the world and are buried on private land upstate.

We do not have social security numbers. We cannot make money or pay taxes, as that would expose our existence. Every transaction is locked inside charitable corporations run by our church—Precious Blood.

To the outside, this arrangement is called organized crime. To us, it's called survival.

From the other side of the black glass that hides me from the driver, I hear a rustling, then a murmur, and my thighs tense until it stops. I can't see the man driving me to my wedding. It doesn't sound like Timothy, who's taken me everywhere since I was small. The voice is deeper, more urgent, and even though I can't make out the words, they're more commanding than a driver's need to be.

My skirt crinkles inside a damp fist.

Sergio will think I have nervous sweats. No man wants a wet-palmed bride. I unclench and smooth the satin before the creases set, then I open the window a crack.

William sees me through the untinted slit and tips his hat with a nod. His silly doorman uniform means nothing to the rest of the world, but we know how important and dangerous his job is. He's one of us. When Daddy moved us to First Avenue, William appeared at the doorman post like a gift.

I roll the window back up.

Peter Colonia emerges. My father's gait is as unhurried as ever, with a loping swerve caused by a club foot. He's taught the world to slow down and wait for him.

With his slicked-back dark hair and otherworldly gold eyes, Daddy doesn't need to be as big as he is to strike fear

7

into men's hearts. How can anyone not fear such unspoken, lethal authority?

William opens the car door, and my father gets in next to me. The door snaps closed. The locks click. The driver pulls away from the curb without another rustle or muffled command.

"Sarah," he says with a voice ravaged by tobacco, leaning back to get the full view of me. "My mother-in-law did all right. You look good."

"Thank you." I touch my hair.

"You nervous?"

There's no use lying to my father.

"Yes."

"You're always one of us." He puts his hand on mine. I can see the old scars at the base of his fingers where he was cut into marriage with my mother. When they locked their hands together, the lines matched. "You got that? Always. No matter what they say."

"Yes, Father."

He regards me with seriousness.

"The Agostis are only a couple of generations from the old country." He takes his hand away. "Not like us. The kids still speak the language like they're running around the streets of Altomonte. So, it's on you to civilize the bastards."

"Yes, Father."

He nods and looks at his phone, then shakes his watch down his wrist and checks the time.

"They're there already," he says, putting his phone away as if he just finished a conversation with my fiancé. "They need this." He snaps his thick fingers, a tic for completion of a thought.

Like many churches in Manhattan, Precious Blood is an unobtrusive building wedged into row housing, only differentiated by the stained glass over the wide brass doors. The windows are boarded from the inside, and no one has entered through the double front doors since we left the Roman Catholic Church in 1888, when they established their own Precious Blood church to compete with ours.

When Daddy told me I was going to marry Sergio Agosti so we could come up from the underground, I asked if we'd open up Precious Blood. He just laughed.

My palms are soaked. I fold them together, but that makes it even worse. I wish I could will my sweat glands to stop leaking.

"You got your gloves?" he asks with a glance at my hands as if he knows the palms have their own water table.

"Yes." I pat my little lace clutch. The gloves go on after I'm cut.

"Agosti's a lucky bastard, you know that?"

"He and Massimo are going to run a big territory."

Daddy smiles with teeth straight and white. He was always proud of his teeth. He said that was how he got such a pretty bride despite his club foot.

"I got something here for you." From his breast pocket, he pulls ziplock bag with lacy fabric pressing against the plastic. "From your mother, for your new husband. She made it when she was still pregnant with you."

He drops it in my lap.

My mother died a long time ago, but she knew this day would come. I'm hesitant to open it—sure some sadness or hope trapped inside will finally be released.

The streets of Manhattan whip by the window, a blurred

melt of sunstruck color lighting up the buildings' gray. We're going down First Avenue instead of taking the FDR. There must be traffic.

"I wish she was here," I say, exerting just enough pressure on the seal to let in air.

"I sent two outsiders to hell for what they did."

"I know." The thought of the outsiders who murdered her stirs up a cloud of hatred.

"Go on," my father says, tapping the bag—maybe encouraging, maybe impatient—looking out the window with concern.

I open the bag and release a circle of lace and elastic.

A garter.

My cheeks flush, and I look down at my dress to hide their color. I finger the soft lace, reveling in the luxury of my dead mother's skill. A little silk disk with a red-and-yellow steam shovel embroidered on it has been tacked to the side. So much detail in such a tiny space. Inside, the words YOU BELONG stitched in red script.

My father looks away, and I know why. After taking off a shoe, I slide the garter up my thigh, under the dress, without exposing myself. This gift could be a mile away from Sergio's fantasies. I have no idea yet what my husband likes. We've met a couple of times. He's handsome and powerful—big in the shoulders and chest, with the wide manner of a man who spent his boyhood in the halls of power.

All I have to do is make him happy. I'm breathless just imagining tonight. The caress of his mouth on my skin. The way my body will please him. A twinge of worry that it won't.

My father frowns as if he senses the filthy turn my thoughts are taking.

Men are easy to read so we don't have to ask a lot of questions.

My grandmother, Marta, drilled this into me, and I'd forgotten to think of my father as no more than a man. So, I read him, and it takes half a moment to realize his frown is directed not at me, but over my shoulder, out the window.

I turn to follow his attention. A shiny black car drives close to us. We've passed First Avenue, driving straight into the sunrise, under the FDR. When I turn back and look over my father's shoulder, I realize we have shiny black neighbors tight on all sides.

For a glancing moment, I panic about being late to my own wedding. The disapproving looks. Sergio's disappointment.

"Sarah," my father murmurs with the tight vocal control he uses when he expects obedience won't be given easily. "Remember what I told you about how to act if you was ever alone with none of us around?" He takes his eyes off the window long enough to meet my gaze. "And some outsiders was asking you questions?"

Why is he bringing this up now?

"Say nothing?"

"You don't scream or give these assholes none of your fear. You stay quiet. We'll send people for you."

"Yes, but—"

"You belong to us. You are Colonia."

"What's happening?"

"*Say it.*" His tone leaves no room for questions.

"I belong to the Colonias."

11

"Good." He snaps his fingers. "Now shut it."

The phalanx of cars veers off the main street and turns sharply into the empty parking lot under the raised highway, stopping so abruptly that my father and I jolt forward.

There's a moment of perfect stillness. Then the partition window that divides us from the driver rolls down, and he turns to us.

I don't know him.

I know everyone I'm supposed to know.

This driver—I can tell he's not one of us. He *looks* like us. Italian, with the last vestiges of a summer tan on olive skin. Dark hair peeking below the driver's cap. A hard jaw with a dusting of angry scruff. Arched black eyebrows over blue eyes that betray a touch of the northern reaches but are dark enough to hide lifetimes of terrible stories.

He's combustible, with an interior so much bigger than his body that it presses against the shell of his skin like an overfull balloon ready to explode.

In fact, he looks as if he wants to rip my father apart, and when he glances at me for a split second of eternity, I fear he may eat me alive just to spite my father.

"Peter Colonia," the man says Daddy's name as if confirming this isn't all a big misunderstanding.

He trains his eyes on me for only a moment longer than he did the first time, and that's all he needs to strip me, shred me bare, rummage through my heart, and find the place I keep the things I deny before I avert my gaze.

This smoldering stranger takes out a gun and points it at Daddy. "This your daughter?"

12

CHAPTER 3

SARAH

IT ISN'T UNTIL DADDY CHUCKLES THAT I FULLY UNDERSTAND THE gravity of our situation.

"Dario fucking Lucari?" My father's question is confirmation.

The man lifts his driver's cap, almost a salute, and places it on the seat next to him. I realize that what I had at first taken for a trick of the light is something else entirely: the tops of his ears are missing. Between the locks of hair is only a flat black line where there should be familiar whorls of skin and cartilage.

I'm certain he'll catch me looking at his disfigurement, but I can't help myself. The unexpectedly missing part makes the whole seem so much more correct.

My father doesn't blink looking down the barrel of a gun. He breathes in the same slow rhythm. He doesn't fear death, and he doesn't crack under pressure. That's why he's our leader.

"Of course you know who I am," Dario sneers.

Behind him, through the windshield, men surround the car. I take my eyes off the driver long enough to look out the side window, where more men approach us. My father impatiently taps a thick, marriage-scarred finger on his knee as if this entire thing is a nuisance.

"Don't puff yourself up. I know every dirtbag operating in this city. It's my business."

My fingers clutch my skirt, and my toes curl in my shoes. My lungs ache in their cage, and that's when I realize I haven't taken a breath since my father demanded silence.

"Your business is sickening," the half-eared man says.

The smirking twitch in his lips plucks a string to my core that has been motionless up until this moment. I try not to wiggle against the tingling in my legs.

My father doesn't respond right away. He just taps the same beat.

"This about money?" my father asks. It's almost a sigh of boredom.

"Everything's about money."

A tremor of relief whispers through me, though I am determined not to let it show. We have plenty of money.

"How much? Just outta curiosity, before my guys get here and hang you like a side of beef."

"No, no, Mr. Colonia. I don't want you to fill my cup. I want my hands on the spigot." Leaning over the seat, the man gets the gun closer to my father's head.

"Kid, you are fucked in the head," Daddy says, slowly shaking his head. "You got enough going on to buy and sell half the shitbags in Manhattan. But this is what you do? How long you been planning to get murdered under the FDR?"

Dario's face flickers with an emotion I can't place, and he turns his attention to me. In a split second, he absorbs the facts of my body and my dress.

Don't cry. I create the words in my mind in my grandmother's voice. *You are Sarah Colonia, and this is your wedding day. You will not arrive at Precious Blood late with ruined makeup.*

You will be beautiful.

You will be pristine.

And you will be given into marriage today.

"How long have I planned this?" Dario asks. "Since the day you fucked up."

My father shifts in his seat, spreading his legs. "I don't fuck up."

Daddy must have more to say than that—some plan, some argument, some *something*—but he doesn't. There's more silence than my heart can bear.

"You forgot," Dario says with a disgusted smile. "Of course you did. It was just another day at the office."

The focus of each man in the car seems to shift out the window, where the scratch of shoes alerts me that something's changed.

Daddy reaches into his jacket for his gun, but Dario redirects his aim to my head and my father freezes.

"Now I'm going to take your daughter."

An exclamatory *hm!* escapes my throat. My vision blurs. Before I can turn, my door opens. Hands grab me. Stars spangle at the edges of the car's dark interior, and I long to be back in that quiet, peaceful moment in the rose gold of the morning sun.

"No!" I scream, resisting. "Stop!"

Even in the blur, the driver's smirk says otherwise, and the tug of anonymous hands trying to get me out of the car suggests I'm wrong.

Another *pop-pop*. A screech. The crackle of breaking glass as the window on my father's side is smashed out, letting in the sun and the cold. I swing hard, fist closed, finding a solid wall of strength. I bite muscle and bone until my teeth feel the crunch of broken skin and my tongue tastes metal.

I've never fought anything so hard in my life, and I'm about to lose when I hear the *whoop-whoop* of a siren.

"Goddamnit," Dario growls from the other side of the universe.

I'm yanked back into my seat as the car takes off. The grabbing hands slide away. The door smacks against a pole, clapping it shut. We're stuck inside a speeding car, and when I look to my father for how to act or what to do, he's not there.

I'm alone with a madman.

His eyes meet mine in the rearview, and I'm chilled by their heat.

"Take it easy back there."

"No." I pull the door handle, but that does nothing. It's locked from the front.

Dario stops short at a light, slaps the car into park, and leans half his body across the seat with his arm extended to press the gun against my belly.

"If I pull this trigger," he whispers, "you won't die. Not right away. You'll just try and stuff your guts back in while I shoot your knees out from under you."

With the gun pressed under my navel and the empty city

16

on view through the broken window, my resistance loses its grace.

"My name is Sarah Colonia," I choke out what I've been trained to say if I was ever separated from my family in the company of outsiders or the authorities. "My father's phone number is—"

"Don't you ever say no to me again." He faces front to drive, putting the gun in his lap. A radio crackles, and he presses a button on a black box. "Status."

"We're clear."

Even though clarity is relayed as if it's a failure, he doesn't seem perturbed. "I'm still in their car. I have her."

"We'll cover you."

"Copy." He tosses the radio aside.

I whimper when he looks at me in the rearview.

"Be quiet, princess." He's demanding but softer as the car drops down a ramp into an underground garage.

With a series of jarring turns, Dario maneuvers around the ramps to the lowest level and parks. He turns to me, cast in half shadow, sharp teeth covered by lips full with soft promise. The edge of the wedding bodice cuts into my breasts as they heave, and my nipples harden under the lace that was meant for my betrothed. I cannot die with my lace underpants wet for my murderer and a corset tied tight for a prince standing alone at an altar.

The doors open. There are men. So many men. One has a needle.

My heart beats faster than a bird's, and my breaths come shallow and fast. I can't get enough air.

"Breathe!" Dario calls from the other side of the spark-edged blackness that takes me.

CHAPTER 4

SARAH

I AM MADE OF WHITE LIGHT.

My eyes blink open, then squeeze shut again. I curl around the pain in my eyes and head. Deep breaths are possible now. The air flows—steady but hitched. Easy, yet constrained. But possible, and essential. So, I take another, and another.

I am Sarah Colonia, and it's my wedding day.

The last thing I remember with any certainty was the car ride to Precious Blood.

What happened to me? I don't feel injured exactly, but I'm sore and achy, not to mention hungry and thirsty. How did I end up in so much pain?

The looseness around my ribs suggests I'm no longer wearing my wedding dress, but my ankles are bare on a hard floor and yards of fabric bunch where my knees bend, suggesting otherwise. My hands are hot, but my fingers aren't, and one side of my face is pressed into soft, uneven fabric.

I've fallen asleep with my head pillowed on the little purse containing my embroidered gloves.

Keeping my eyes closed, I touch where the seams have left tender grooves in my cheek and then my dry, chapped lips. I can tell just by feel that my hair is a lost cause; the morning's perfect updo, constructed by Grandma before the sun rose, has dissolved into a disheveled wreck. Could this all be the result of a long, late party? Did I have too much to drink and manage to forget the day I've been waiting for?

I search for memories of my fiancé's face when we were cut, of the food at the reception, the dancing, the singing of old Italian songs I can pronounce but don't understand.

I am not cut. There was no wedding. No Sergio.

What can I expect from him? The marriage deal was made after his father met me at Armistice Night. The negotiations were made without me. Then I met him at one of our grand houses uptown. I remember the way he watched me, sizing me up—deciding if I was worth marrying for the underground kingdom of Manhattan. I held my head high because I am a daughter of the Colonia, and he's barely two generations from savagery.

As I was walking from the kitchen to the dining room to clear the plates, Sergio stole a moment, pushing me into the hall, his breath on me, the weight of his hand between my breasts.

"No," I hissed. He pushed me harder. "Please."

He backed up. "Say no to me when we're married, lady-girl. See where that gets you."

I had no intention of refusing after the wedding. But I had no intention of letting him ruin me before that either.

My hands continue their path down my body, checking

now for blood or scars, evidence of real, serious violence—whatever happened that I wasn't awake to remember.

There's no soreness between my legs, which is the final bit of proof that I am still intact.

And I am... where, exactly?

Gathering my courage, I carefully open my eyes, blinking until they adjust to the blinding light, focusing it into black-outlined rectangles, squares, shapes gone rhomboid from the distortion of perspective.

The shapes are glass panes, and the dark outlines are the casings between them.

Winter sunlight falls in dazzling streaks through the dusty panes. The sun is nearly directly overhead, which makes it close to noon. I've been dumped into a greenhouse, where I've been out for half a day.

I sit up and gingerly get to my feet, but the world tips over. I land on my hands and knees.

If I can't walk, I'll crawl.

The floor is cracked tile, grouted with decades of dirt. I push past a green plastic nursery pot with hairy soil stuck to the sides. A flat yellow stick with a flower genus printed on the side.

Plant in full sun six weeks before last frost. Space seeds 4-6".
Sprouts will emerge in 5-17 days. Keep soil moist until 6" tall.

My head feels as if it has a brick wired to each side, pressing down against my skull, forcing blood and fluid through the veins.

Against the wall, at the top of a pipe that juts from the floor, sits a brass spigot with a foot of black hose attached.

With my dry mouth stuck shut, I reach for the webbed circle at the top. Turn it.

Nothing comes.

Approaching a counter with two empty shelves under it, I have to remind myself through the headache that I'm alive. I can reach for the bottom shelf. I can feel the cold steel. I can get my feet under me. I can pull myself up high enough to lean on the second shelf, and when my stomach cramps from hunger and a bodice that isn't as tightly strung as I remember, I can feel every organ in my body and close my eyes against the pain.

I'm alive, but why?

In the blessed darkness behind closed lids, I pull myself to a standing position.

Slowly, I open my eyes, and I am flying. There's no ground outside the windows. No street. No pavement. Nothing nearby. Only a ledge, then a horizon cracked into the geometry of the city, and from this, I get my bearings.

I'm in a rooftop greenhouse several stories higher than the nearest buildings. The place doesn't seem to be in use. The few metal shelves and racks are mostly empty, save for the occasional stack of trays or flowerpots, a stray bag of soil moldering on the tile.

Manhattan is spread out around me on three sides, laid out as if it's within reach.

Northeast. Central Park, night wildness inside the right angles of floodlit green frame.

Empire State Building. South and east.

Chrysler Building. Less south. More east.

Brooklyn, then the rest of the island disappearing into

the haze of Montauk and the Atlantic Ocean, to my ancestral home, Venice, where the bubonic plague raged.

I am west of Times Square and a little north, twelve stories above the smutty grind of Hell's Kitchen.

The structure's built against the exit of a building, and there's a door. Solid, flush at the edges with no molding. It's even painted the same color as the wall, as if it's supposed to be incongruous.

I'm not surprised when it's locked, but I'm frustrated.

I turn the knob. Pull. Yank. Leverage my foot against the wall as if muscle and bone can beat a deadbolt

"Hey!" I pound the metal. "Hey! Driver guy!"

He has a name.

Dario Lucari.

I won't say his name.

I punch the door as hard as I can, screaming with every bit of air I can fit inside my lungs, and pound harder. Shocks of pain rattle my wrists and the sides of my hands burn from the friction. I'm going to break a bone, shatter my insides, bash them to jelly before I even find out what happened.

Maybe that's for the best.

Maybe that's what needs to be.

Or maybe this is pointless. I push myself away from the door and go back to the east-facing side of the greenhouse.

I can see the building on First Avenue where we've lived since Mommy died.

Can palms on the cold glass communicate with home when our windows face east and away? Home has its back turned to the princess trapped alone in a tower.

Stepping back, I search for a door in the glass and find it, but it's locked tight. I yank the cast-iron lever anyway. It's that move that demonstrates how loose my dress is around me, the corseted top that should be sculpted against my ribs now a loose raft of fabric and boning. I reach for the laces that should be keeping me secure and realize with a start that they were taken while I was unconscious. No wonder it's so easy to breathe.

Why would they take the lacing? For better access to my body. I can't think of another reason.

I take another step back and pick up one of the pots, a terracotta thing with some heft to it, and throw it against the greenhouse glass with all my might.

The pot shatters on impact, and the window absorbs the blow with a dull, disinterested thud.

I throw another, then another, watching them explode, splintering uselessly into fragments and dust. I shriek a sob of rage and fear, and the sound startles me—I clap my hands over my mouth.

You don't scream or give these assholes none of your fear.

My father told me to be silent.

You belong to us.

I'd forgotten.

You are Colonia.

No one comes, and for a moment, Daddy's instructions are a mercy.

Then I'm confronted with the cyclops gaze of a camera I hadn't noticed before. It's mounted in a corner, too high to reach, its lens shiny and black, as menacing as the view down the barrel of a gun. Next to it, a red light blinks.

Whoever they are, they're watching me closely.

I've always known we have enemies. Other, newer families calling themselves Mafia or *Cosa Nostra*. They are criminals, and the few authorities we aren't inside confuse us with them. But until now, that knowledge remained vague and shadowy—as I got older, I started to think of our rivals as nothing more than bogeymen the grandmothers used to keep little girls in line.

Of course, the outside people would destroy our way of life if they knew about it—but they don't know about it. How could they? We are stealthy and smart. Law-abiding citizens, invisible in the system for generations. We're nothing more than a web of imperceptible connections.

I look for something to hide under—a table, a chair, a pile of burlap, anything to shield me from that impassive, all-seeing gaze. But there's nothing: just empty racks and broken pots and my ruined dress hovering inches from my as-yet-unruined body.

I press the neckline to the skin and look right at the camera. "Are you just a pervert?"

Nothing happens. I bend my knee to take off my shoe, grab it by the toe, and as my arm is back, I think of the times Grandma took me out and all the outsider men who looked at me with lust.

"Pathetic." I fling the shoe at the camera and hit it, but it still stares at me.

It's not until night, with hunger clawing my body from the stabbing in my guts to the tingle in my fingers that I hear footsteps from the other side of the door. Even through the hope of food and rescue, I back away from it.

The door to the greenhouse bangs open. I whirl around to find myself once again face-to-face with Dario Lucari.

CHAPTER 5

SARAH

DARIO'S NOW DRESSED IN PLAIN CLOTHES: DARK PANTS AND A white shirt with buttons open at the throat. The sleeves are rolled up to reveal his tattooed forearms. They are corded with muscle, and the rest of him coils like a whip. He's tall and deceptively slender. I don't think I stand a chance if I attack him outright. Especially since the cold façade he presented in the car has cracked open to reveal a simmering cruelty that scares me more than anything.

"Princess Colonia," he says without an ounce of emotion. He's stating a fact, and I am that fact.

You don't give these assholes none of your fear.

"Only daughter of Peter Colonia, one of the most powerful crime families in all of New York."

"Don't talk about us like that. We're not like you." I don't know what he's like, but we wouldn't point a gun at a woman's head on her wedding day.

He takes a couple of steps in my direction, stopping in a strip of blue moonlight.

"You went to a private school in an abandoned church. All your friends were raped into marriage in their teens. Your life was sold for territory." He spits out the last word.

One of the first things a Colonia child learns is how to deny her world if outsiders ask. I respond automatically, my voice surprisingly proud for someone who's shaking in her skin.

"I don't know what you're talking about."

His laugh is mirthless. "Don't lie to me."

I remember the feeling of the gun at my head, his look of determination, the way a potential for violence seeped from his pores, stinging my nose with bitter terror and the sense that I'd never been so alive.

He knows about us, and he means us harm.

And yet he is like a vaccine, inoculating me against fear by giving me a dose of it.

"Do you feel pathetic?" he asks.

I bow my head so my face doesn't give me away.

"You should," he continues with a sneer. "You're neither as powerful, nor as pure as you think."

I remain silent.

"You think your little group, your secret society, will protect you. That it cares about you. You believe that it *matters* to be among the chosen."

He's drawn close to me, but he doesn't touch me. The malice radiating off him is as palpable to me as his body heat.

"It's my wedding day," I say to the floor because I need to say something and it's the one thing he knows already.

"I don't have any sympathies," he assures me. "So, if

you're trying to appeal to them, you can save your energy. You'll need it."

My eyes settle on the hollow of his throat, near where his pulse throbs, and I think. *Okay*. He can claim he has no human side, but he is fully corporeal. Just a man.

"You want something from my father." I look up, meeting his eyes. "He'll give it to you. Whatever it is."

My father would draw the stars down from the sky for me. I'm as sure of this as I am of gravity.

"What if I want something from *you*?" Dario asks with a gaze so direct I'm lifted from the floor, standing on nothing but air and the solidness of his will.

It's unbearable. When I try to put my own gaze back on the floor, he takes me by the chin and points it up until I'm looking right into the dark emptiness of his eyes.

"I know what you want," I say. His hand falls away from my face, and I make an effort to point it upward without his help. "It's the only thing you can take from me."

"Maybe I just want a forbidden plaything."

"My family will find you."

"Correct. The minute I made that first wrong turn, I was as good as dead. Shit, the minute I put your driver in the hospital, I committed to my own murder. But enough about me. Let's talk about you and how much you mean to me."

"They won't let you hurt me."

He scoffs as if I've said something laughably naïve. "They'll let me torture and abuse you before I kill you, as long as their hive isn't disrupted. They'll let you die to maintain secrecy. They'll let me stick my cock anywhere I want if it'll buy them time." He shakes his head and takes one step back. "If, in your worthless education, they taught you the world was fair, they lied to you."

"Just do it, then." I stop holding up my dress. It doesn't drop but sits inches away from my body. The cold air goose-bumps my breasts where the loosened bodice falls away. "I can't stop you."

"Be quiet, *Schiava.*"

I don't know what the last word means. Maybe it's Italian. My family came here at least two hundred years before his showed up. Civilization has wiped the language from my genetic code.

Dario circles me, taking in my dusty dress and single shoe, making it clear that he'd just as soon spit on me as have to keep looking at me.

"I'm not one of you, and that's all that you need to know. I don't follow your rules. I don't honor your boundaries. I don't care how many hundreds of years of uninterrupted triumph you've enjoyed. I have my own people, and they follow my rules. To the letter. Or I shoot them."

My heart is a fist trying to punch its way out.

"Nod if you understand," he says.

I nod. I understand he's a murderous deviant. That's enough.

"*Bene, principessa,*" he says, and I take it for an agreement.

"I'm not a princess," I insist. "If that's what you mean to call me."

"No, you're not a princess to them. You're a tool. Or..." He takes half a step back to take in the whole of my frame. "A nail. Just another pretty little nail holding up the entire structure."

He doesn't deserve my denial because he'll only use it to prove his point. If he wants to rape me, he will. I press my lips together. He doesn't say anything, stretching the silence between us until his attention is so taut my insides squirm.

"I know what they tell you," he says before breaking his gaze to come behind me. I feel him there. I feel how my dress hovers away from me. Feel his eyes probe in the space between, looking for the place the shadows cast my body into mystery. "That you're separate. That you don't hurt anyone. That you have your own economy with the outside and it runs clean. That it's moral. That you're sheltered for your own protection. I've met plenty who know what they tell you. I never met anyone stupid enough to believe it."

I feel his breath on my skin, and I want him to touch me so badly I have to swallow back a plea.

"I'm not stupid," I snap defensively.

Outsider men live for nothing besides themselves. They consume a woman's soft parts and discard the husks on the street. Grandma told me horror stories when I was little— tales of what depraved men have done to women who leave the Colonia. Seduced by promises of love or money or freedom, they're destroyed by all three.

Then it happened to my mother. She wasn't seduced. She was out getting fabric, and she was forced. I hate these men. One of them raped and killed my mother.

"How do you know so much about us?" I ask, distracting myself from the heat of his body and his animal scent. I'm facing east, turned in the direction of the apartment building that has its back turned on me. If I can keep my attention there, I won't fall to my knees.

"How I know is irrelevant." His voice and breath move

from one shoulder to the next as if he's stroking me with a fingertip. "Ask me *what* I know, and I can spend all day telling you about you." He pauses, and I'm convinced he's going to touch me. "I know that you haven't had anything to eat or drink since sundown yesterday."

The afternoon sunlight is making me sweat, a clammy thing that spreads at the backs of my knees and my neck as my pulse hammers too hard in my wrists.

"You're a monster," I whisper.

"And you look beautiful in that dress."

I hate him for saying it, and I hate myself for being pleased that he means it.

As he steps away, a piece of clay pot crackles under his heel. For the first time since I broke the pots, I realize that the pieces are sharp enough to shear skin and soft vascular tissue.

Dario stands to my right and pushes a shard away with the toe of his shoe.

I could kill myself. End it all. Remove the possibility of him finding my weaknesses or raping them out of me. Whatever Dario wants from us, he wants it badly enough to kidnap me. If I'm his only leverage and I remove myself from the equation, he won't get what he wants.

"You broke the pot you were supposed to shit in." He flicks the shard away. It skips and clicks a few feet, landing on top of another one and transferring its energy until they both take off in opposite directions.

"I need water," I say.

"I know." He's in profile—not fully turned to me—when he says it, and I can see where the top of his ear ends in a surgically straight line.

Turning away, he opens the door just enough for me to see light on the other side, then he slips through and closes it behind him.

The deadbolt clicks. I drop to my knees and weep, and the sadness sedates me into something that I mistake for sleep.

CHAPTER 6

DARIO

SOMEWHERE IN QUEENS, THE TOWN CAR IS GETTING STRIPPED down to the chassis and disassembled like a Colonia bride on her wedding night. Missing the car switch was a contingency we'd planned for. We weren't followed. Oliver and Tamara, my heads of security, made sure of that. Everything to plan.

So, why am I sitting alone in a dark room, trying to figure out what went wrong?

In the car, she caught me off guard.

Bronze hair swept off her shoulders in a perfect twist, in her corseted wedding gown, wide brown eyes with explosions of amber at the centers.

My brother, Nico, is a facts-on-the-ground guy. He's not prone to under- or overstatement, so when he told me Sarah Colonia turned out nice looking, I believed him. Figured he was describing a girl somewhere in the bell curve of fuckability. A girl you'd make an effort to get into bed but not one you'd wait around for. Someone else's wife. You'd understand how another guy wanted her for the rest of his life but not why. Or you'd understand why but not how.

Beauty isn't new. That's not it.

Oliver's a refrigerator-sized man with a boyish face that belies years spent fighting foreign wars. He clears his throat. "Sir? Is anything wrong with the setup?"

"No."

"Should we give her a few blankets?"

"No."

"Tamara's working on a secure line to the Colonia."

My watch beeps in a familiar rhythm. *One-two, one-two-three. One-two, one-two-three.* I shut it.

"Is there something on your mind, Ollie?"

"We usually follow a different protocol."

"She's not usual."

I leave before he questions me again. In a smaller room, I open a hidden cabinet with a small flat screen behind it. It's for one thing—one person—only.

A minute later, it comes to life.

Nico appears from somewhere under Precious Blood, secretly embedded with the Colonia technical data crew.

The screen he sees me in reflects on his big, wire-rimmed glasses. We have the same parents, but while I got our asshole father's dark, wavy hair and blue eyes, he got our mother's dirty-blond ringlets and tobacco eyes.

"Tell me everything," I demand in a tone that's curious, not furious.

"It was beautiful," he replies from deep inside enemy territory. "She was 'late,' and for the first twelve and a half minutes, Giovanni Agosti went on and on about Midtown traffic while his son tried telling jokes from the pulpit."

"And when he realized he was ditched?"

"It was..." Nico shudders. "Scary. Even from up in the nosebleed seats..."

"Prince Charming isn't so charming."

"Don't count on his tail staying between his legs. How's his betrothed?"

"Better off, she just doesn't know it yet."

"She may never know it," he says. "She was groomed to be a king's wife."

"It'll take me forty-eight hours to get her heeling and begging for a biscuit."

"My point is, she's not like the rest of them."

That's for sure. She's not broken. Yet.

"She's not exactly good looking," I reply.

"Really?"

"She's stunning."

The shit that comes out of my mouth surprises Nico, and if I'm being honest for a change, it even shocks me.

"Has it finally happened?" he asks. "Are you getting moony?"

"Have I ever mooned over a woman?"

"You're due."

If he ever sees the day, he'll drop dead. So will I.

"That part of me died," I say.

"All the more reason you might fall for a woman you can't keep."

Once Nico fell in love, the fact that I never have and never will started bugging him. Like I've gotta be his emotional mirror.

"Forget what I'm doing," I say. "What are *they* doing?"

"Trying to figure out what you know. But keeping Sergio

from setting the whole town on fire is sucking away a lot of the energy for now. We have a week, tops, before they start calling in favors at the sheriff's department."

"Are you close to getting Tamara her hookup?"

"Yeah. We're ready."

"It's time to throw them off. Give them a reason to make a mistake."

It takes us twenty minutes to calibrate the practicality and brutality of our next move.

GOD WATCHES OVER EVERYTHING, but He's not going to tap you on the shoulder and tell you what He sees. God doesn't fill out and file shift reports. He lays the roads and paves the streets. He digs the tunnels and levels the mountains. He keeps the skyscrapers standing, making the laws of physics consistent enough to fool us into believing the system is reliable.

How you travel those grids and occupy those buildings is up to you.

God formed the infrastructure of the physical world, then we created flawed tools to understand how we fit into it, making sure some people didn't quite fit at all.

She's better off. She just doesn't know it yet.

Fuck those tools. I made my own... except now I'm not sure what they've built.

She was groomed to be a king's wife.

Oliver's home with his wife. I'm alone in my windowless security room, where two walls of screens show me every moment of every entrance to every space in every property I

35

own. Blind corners. Narrow halls. Nondescript doors. Drained of color and detail, they could be anywhere in the city, but I know them like lovers no other man desires because they've never been intimate with them. Only I've taken the time to know the shape of that crack in the pavement, the proportion of the spacing between the doors, the growth rate of the tree at the edge of the sidewalk.

The trick to this job isn't to look at any one screen, but to see all of them until one changes, then observe how that change affects the spaces around it. Sometimes the change is a break in the motion, a reduced tempo, or a quirk in the way one person travels from corner to corner.

But it's late, and the activity on most of the screens is tranquil.

She's not like the rest of them.

Only one has my attention. Only one distracts me from the overall rhythm. That screen is the reason I dismissed the two men in here.

Sarah's separated two layers of her skirt, placing one between her torso and the cold floor and the other under her legs. Her head rests on her wrists, which are covered by white gloves.

She's not broken.

The greenhouse was meant to be uncomfortable for Peter Colonia's daughter.

He ruined our lives. He destroyed our mother with a flick of his wrist.

He did it for his own comfort because the Colonia gave him the power to do it.

The only limits to what I'd do to cause him pain are the

boundaries of my own anger and intelligence. Killing him would be a failure of imagination.

We plan to destroy the one thing he loves—the Colonia —through the one person he groomed to sustain it.

She's not broken. Yet.

I press a button on the console, and the greenhouse screen flips to thermal imaging. Everything is blue and cold except for a bright rainbow where she lies—centered with a bright red bean ringed in orange, then yellow following the curve of her sleeping body.

She's fine for now. The hot core of her soul is keeping her alive.

When it cools, she'll be a little closer to where I want her.

Broken.

CHAPTER 7

SARAH

THE SECOND TIME I WAKE UP IN THE GREENHOUSE, IT'S DARK. MY legs are cold, and at some point in my unconscious state, I must have taken off my gloves because my hands are free. My joints ache, and my entire head hurts. I'm hours past hunger pangs. A mass of glue and sand has lodged itself in my throat.

The minutes crawl into hours while my vision gets used to the light. I spot one of my gloves resting by my shoe, and it's not until I reach for it that I realize my skirt's hitched over my knees.

Did he...?

No. He didn't.

He isn't interested in raping me. He's interested in watching me starve.

Leaning forward for the glove, I check the camera. The red light glows steadily.

Dario hadn't been speaking lightly when he threatened my survival, but it wasn't pure sadism. Torturing me is a sideshow. He's after something bigger. I'm just a nail holding up a bigger plan.

The only way to keep him from getting what he wants is to take myself out of the negotiations. Just then, my eyes adjust to the shapes on the tile. He removed my laces to keep me from killing myself, but he left the shards.

Well, that was his mistake.

After grabbing the glove, I gather my skirts, slyly picking up a triangle of pottery to tuck into the base of my palm. To mask what I'm doing from the camera, I put the glove back on while—under the fabric—I tuck the pointy side of the shard into my wrist. Once I cut it open, all I have to do is curl up and bleed out. They won't notice until I'm already dead. They can't stop me, and they'll lose. We'll survive.

My starving brain decides it's a good plan—until the edge of the ceramic is pressed to my skin.

What if suicide helps his plan? If I don't know his intentions, I could fall right into his trap.

Pressing the shard into my glove, flat side against my skin, I decide not to use it until I can be sure it's the best way to hurt him.

So, I find the warmest part of the greenhouse, over a hot-air vent, and watch the sun come up over the Atlantic.

My thoughts degrade into colors weaving together. Fear is green and yellow. Thirst is brown and burgundy. They become a whirring, spinning loom that clatters as it twists them together. I sleep tangled in them.

HOVERING BETWEEN SLEEP AND CONSCIOUSNESS, I dream of life when this is over.

First, eat like a pig for a year. This dress won't fit around the pasta and soft cheese.

Every day I'll drink a pot of espresso and eat a plate of pastries. *Tricolore* and *sfogliatella* and the cookies with the nuts on top. And sausages. Miles of them.

Food is all I've ever known of the old country, and now it's all I can think about. Rich sauces with cloves and braised meats. Bowls of olives in shades of brown and green and red, with enough salty brine to sting puckered lips.

And water.

Gallons and gallons of water.

When I can't think of water another moment, I spend my energy on hope. I have not been ruined. Not even touched. Daddy will believe me. He'll convince Sergio and the Agosti family to continue with the marriage. I cling to that fantasy as the endless hours unfold.

But every time I try to reassure myself with this thought, another set of memories comes rushing in: half-remembered snatches of gossip, tales of women who *had* ruined themselves, as if that treasure was theirs to spend.

I find another pot to pee in, but nothing's gone in, so little comes out.

The sun slips below the horizon, and in the night's darkness, I try to sleep. Rest is fitful, uneven, and my dreams are all nightmares of Grandma's disappointment. She tells me it's all right, blinking out when I try to touch her, only to reappear far away. Just before dawn breaks, I'm trapped in a feverish delusion of being stuck in a tunnel, punishing darkness enclosing me, surrounded by the skittering sounds of rats and madmen.

I'm half mad myself by the time the moon crawls over New Jersey, shimmering down brilliantly at me from a night sky the color of a just-erased blackboard.

How can I still be here? I clutch the sharp piece of pottery under my glove. It's a safety blanket. A choice I can make in a situation where my decisions are meaningless.

Hovering in half consciousness, my eyes are closed when the door bangs open again and Dario enters, carrying a tall glass of water. He sets it on a dirty counter in front of me, then leans against the table, crossing one long leg over the other.

I get to my feet and approach the glass, wary but unable to stay away from it. I've never been this thirsty in my life; my eyeballs burn, and my tongue's cracked into layers of plaster.

Dario watches me silently, but as I reach out to take the glass, he slaps my hand away. I'm already weak and dizzy, and the force of the blow makes me stumble and spin.

"Please!" I cry. I realize I'm on my knees. I had intended to be strong, to refuse to let him see me suffer any more, but I am so, so thirsty.

"Take that stupid dress off."

I shake my head. I'm past caring about modesty. I care about the dress. It's ruined, but it's mine. I worked on it for months, my fingers numb from stitching, my eyes and back aching as I labored into the night. It may be the only piece of home left to me besides my own body, and I will not take it off.

He shrugs and picks up the glass of water.

I remain defiant.

He turns to go.

And when I feel the triangle of clay inside the wrist of my glove, I think, with blinding clarity, *I cannot die here.*

"Okay," I say.

He stops, turns around, but does not put down the glass.

I slip the dress off slowly, regretfully, because as awful as it looks, the fabric is still fine, soft and sweet, a reminder of who I was and what I expected so few sunrises ago. The gloves stay and so do the undergarments I wore to please Sergio because Dario just said to take off the dress and I'm weak but not dead. I'm not giving him anything he doesn't ask for.

He places the glass back on the table. Then he sweeps a hand through the dust and dirt on its surface and sprinkles them into the water. I watch helplessly as it clouds over in the moonlight.

"Down to the skin," he says. "Show me every inch."

The suggestion in his command floods my dry veins with resistance.

"You said the dress." I hold out my left hand—the one without the distorting piece of pottery under the glove. "Give it to me."

This time, he takes a discarded nursery container and pinches out white-flecked potting soil. He drops it in the water like a chef seasoning too heavily.

"It's going to be mud soon," he says. "If you aren't naked."

"Where's my father?" I squeak without spit. "Did he give you what you want?"

"Haven't spoken to him since the car."

"I don't believe you."

"We tried. He won't negotiate with outsiders... so... take off *all* your fucking clothes."

I do everything I can not to keep from crying as I lower my white lace underpants and slip out of my matching bra, hands shaking the entire time. I leave the gloves and garter, hoping they're beside the point.

"I know what you're hiding in your glove. You're not going to kill me with a broken flowerpot."

"It wasn't for you."

He nods with understanding but not compassion, as if knowing suicide is on the table adds to a data point and no more, then flicks his finger at me. I peel off the gloves. The shard clatters to the floor. I am now naked except for one thing.

"The garter."

"Not that." I ball my hands into fists and look at the floor. "Please."

He says nothing. I can't see him, so I let myself hope that he's considering letting me keep this one strip of fabric and elastic that's tying me to this earth, to my identity, to the one person who loved me like no other. Maybe he'll find it arousing.

I'll risk it, even embrace it, for that glass of cloudy water.

The sound of a *plop* and a splash catches my attention, and I look up to see him slowly pouring a thin line of water onto the tile.

With a gasp, thoughts of my mother are gone, and I rip off the garter before I lose another precious drop, throwing it at his feet.

CD REISS

"There," I say, finally bare before him, exposed as I have never been before a man.

My breath skips, and I finally cry, but I don't have enough water in my body to make tears or snot over this destroyed moment—the first time a man's eyes see my skin, my nipples, my utter vulnerability.

The moment I took that dress off was supposed to be one of the most beautiful of my life. Instead, it is a violation.

He isn't satisfied yet though.

"Stay still," he commands.

He walks behind me, hovering for a moment before grabbing my hair and yanking it back so that I'm gazing up into the camera's merciless eye.

"Can you imagine how good it will feel," he murmurs, his breath hot against my neck, "when I let you drink?" He lays his other hand under my chin and slides it down as he speaks. "That cold, sweet water sliding down your throat?"

I nod helplessly, gulping what feels like a lump of garden pebbles.

"Even with a little dirt, a little dust, you'll take it all down, won't you? You're just about ready to beg for it."

"I'll beg," I agree with a voice I don't recognize. "I'll do it."

"You need it," he says, and I can *feel* the cruelty of the smile in his voice.

"Please," I whisper. "Please... please..."

"Say it for the camera."

Who's on the other side? His boss? My family? The entire world?

"Please give it to me."

"Let me swallow it," he whispers thickly. "Beg."

44

"Let... let me swallow it all. Please."

"I know what your body needs. And what you'll do to get it."

And then, just as abruptly as he'd grabbed me, he spins me around so that I'm facing him and he pushes me to my knees.

"This will go much easier for you if you play along," he murmurs.

I'm so weak and dizzy I almost tip over before he pulls me up by the hair on top of my head.

"Steady, *principessa*." With his free hand, he opens the fly of his pants, exposing the thick bulge beneath cotton underwear.

He's going to take it out and force me to taste his cock. Take it down my throat. Swallow his come.

I've spent my life waiting for this, and I don't want it this way... but I want it. My body aches to just give up, taste whatever he puts on my tongue. I look up at him, offering whatever he's willing to take as long as he gives me something to drink.

But he does not release his erection.

Instead, he pulls my head into his crotch. The fabric is damp on my lips, heavy and musty on my nose as he grinds into my face. And he's hard. So hard. He forces the shape of his shaft along the opening between my lips, and I taste no more than an essence of him... but it's enough. My clit fills and drops, weighted by a constant, brutal pulse of arousal that's timed to the way he pushes into my face, holding my head still.

My hands steady me against his thighs, then pull him closer.

I want it.

I surrender.

I'll suck him for water or a glass of sand.

Why is he keeping it behind his clothes?

"Yes," he growls, putting both hands behind my head and pushing me into his crotch so hard his erection feels like stone on my chin.

I put out my tongue, licking the damp fabric. He stops for a moment. His growl turns into a gasp, and the clothed organ against me pulses. A warm wetness gathers at my cheek.

Then he lets me go, and I fall back on my hands, gasping as I notice the thick wet stain where he came as I licked him.

"Okay," he says, zipping up. He's bored again, casual as he hands the glass to me by the top. "You can drink now."

I do. I am shameless and desperate. I hold it with both hands and savor every drop, dirt and all.

He leaves before I finish, apparently not interested in watching me debase myself further.

I lie naked where he left me, legs in the letter K, bare skin on cold tile, the empty glass a few inches from my hand, watching the clouds form in the grid above me.

The door clicks and whooshes open. The room spins when I bolt to a sitting position. A tray of food, accompanied by a whole pitcher of water, is pushed across the threshold.

The door claps shut again, and the deadbolt is smacked home.

I glance at the camera. He's watching. He has to be.

I should stand up and walk like a human, but by the time I finish making that decision, I'm already crawling on my hands and knees like an animal.

The tray contains a plastic clamshell with a sandwich inside—pink meat spills from a circle of bread split into a pocket. Hushing the raging hunger for a moment, I peek into the pocket and find cheese and the familiarity of mayonnaise. A pink container of yogurt proudly proclaims—next to a bulbous strawberry—that it has REAL FRUIT inside.

I rip it open, ready to suck it down, but I stop.

I stand carefully, my head still swimming not just from my hunger and thirst and poor night's sleep, but from what just happened. I walk over to my discarded pile of garments and put them on again: the underwear and bra, the ruined dress, my shoes—one close by and one under the camera. I slide the garter up my leg.

I leave the gloves and shard.

Then I put the tray on the counter, right a white plastic chair that matches the one on the roof, and—dressed in silk garments that were once a hopeful symbol of my purity but are now nothing more than a painful, ridiculous reminder of everything I have lost—I hydrate and nourish myself, dreaming of the day I escape the man named Dario with shadow eyes and an empty heart.

47

CHAPTER 8

SARAH

THE CRIPPLING FEAR THAT HAD GRIPPED ME GIVES WAY TO A constant, numbing unease, a prickling that won't quite leave my skin. I wonder how long it will take to make my isolation unremarkable.

I sleep deeply that night, too exhausted for anything else, but I wake with the sunrise and spend the day pacing circles around the greenhouse, looking for something— anything, really. A clue. An escape hatch. A needle and thread so I can turn this ridiculous gown into something practical. I read the instructions on the back of the bag of potting soil, hoping that whoever's on the other side of the camera will take the hint and deliver a book, but they don't.

Mostly though, I watch the human specks on the slices of street I can see. The klatches of smokers on balconies. The cars crawling along the rivulet avenues. Airplanes. A light on the twenty-third floor of a building on 38th Street flicking off. The ferries crossing the Hudson like loose teeth in a watery mouth.

The rest of the world is so close—and completely untouchable.

People. Outsiders. Doing things. Going places. Worrying. Dreaming. Thinking thoughts. All while I watch from above, wondering what their lives are like.

And wonder.

And wonder as if for the first time, but it's not. From my sheltered life, I've always wondered, and now I'm in a glass tower, ignorant but still harboring curiosities that will never be satisfied.

Inside the walls that kept the city's chaos at bay, I was happy. I knew who I was and what I was intended for, even if I was curious about the things I saw in store windows or snatches of conversation I overheard. Now I'm stranger to the world, imagining a life outside a box that's landed on a planet I've only seen through a telescope.

The cloud-cloaked sun sits at the top of the sky when there's a knock at the door. The noise doesn't startle me as much as the courtesy. Would Dario knock before raping or killing me?

I hear murmurs behind the door. Two men. I creep up to listen.

"She's not gonna be, like, 'Come on in, guys.'"

"What am I supposed to do? Bust in? What if she's on the pot or something"

Neither one is Dario.

"Do like the doctor's office. Knock and open at the same time."

"That's my point. Doctors are fucking scary."

Are they trying not to scare me?

"Jesus fucking..." The rest sounds like a litany of curses in

Italian until he raises his voice and calls clearly through the door. "Uh, Miss Colonia, we got your lunch."

"See," says the other voice. "Now you're asking permission."

"*Porca miseria.*" The door gets three hard pounds. "We're coming in."

The deadbolt snaps, and I realize I'm going to get hit by the door just in time to get out of the way.

Two men in suits enter. Both of them are looming and intense—men who know violence intimately, who take it into their beds each night like a beloved wife, and yet they're more human than Dario. Fallible. Flawed. One is middle-aged with a receding hairline and a growing paunch. He holds a lunch tray with another clamshell-encased sandwich, a bottle of water, and juice box. The other is in his thirties, over six feet tall with a full head of black hair and large brown eyes. He closes the door and stands in front of it.

I must look a sight because the younger man shakes his head in pity.

"It's all right." He holds up his hands to show me they're empty.

"Says you." The other one scoffs. "We brought you lunch." He puts the tray on a table. "It ain't much, but pretend it's something because you got five minutes to eat it."

"Why?" I look from one to the other.

They don't talk like they're from here, yet there's something familiar about them.

"'Cos the guy paying us says you gotta eat, then come

downstairs. No trouble or there's gonna be trouble." He leaves the tray and stands at the door.

I approach, open the water, and put it to my lips. They're watching me. Drinking in front of them is uncomfortable, but I'm parched and finish the bottle.

"You both were there when he took me. You were outside—"

"Yeah," the tall one says. "We were there."

"We're sorry about how that went down."

Tall elbow-jabs Short in the arm hard enough to send him off balance, then says, "Eat up."

I crack open the clamshell. "You have names?"

"I'm Gennaro," the short guy says.

"Give her your address, why don't you?"

"Like I'm the only Gennaro."

"Jesus Christ."

"She's not gonna believe your mother named you that." Gennaro addresses me, "This asshole's name is Vito."

"Nice to meet you both." I'm only half lying. These two are not soft. I'm sure they'd hurt me at the first sign of trouble, but they do not belong here. "I... um... all that water? I have to use the pot."

"We'll wait outside," Vito says. "Two and a half minutes, then we go. No trouble. We're not gonna like dragging you down the stairs, but we will."

I have no doubt he's telling the truth, and I nod my understanding. They leave.

As I squat, I realize the door opens inward. When they almost hit me as they entered, I dodged right. If I'd dodged left, I would have been hidden behind the door.

If I just had a way to draw them in, I could slip behind them.

With little time to waste, I reach under my skirt, grab the lining, and bite the edge, creating a little notch. I rip along the weft, then the wale, ignoring the voice that asks what I think I'm going to do on the other side of that door. The rest of the building has to be guarded. I'll never make it to the first floor.

As I rip off the last few inches of fabric, there's a soft knock.

"Ms. Colonia," Vito says before the deadbolt snaps open.

I throw the white silk to the center of the room and run behind the door.

It's going to work. It's stark white, and for a split second, a decent person could think I've collapsed.

"What the—?" Gennaro runs in. Three steps in, and he's halfway there.

Vito has his gun out. He doesn't rush in as fast. Half a step and I slip behind him, clutching my bodice closed so the entire dress doesn't fall away, into a windowless, beige foyer.

I'm relieved by the change in scenery and terrified, lost, hopeless as I grab the painted pipe handrails and aim my feet for the grip tape on the edges of the concrete steps.

"Come on, man." Vito's voice is so close to me I know I was never even close to escaping.

Gennaro arrives in the background, clutching a handful of white fabric, and jokingly asks, "Where did you think you were going?"

Besides these stairs, there's nowhere to go. I was going wherever they were taking me.

"You coming or not?" I ask.

Vito jogs ahead, Gennaro stays behind, and we descend the stairs.

That escape attempt was a disaster, but it won't be my last. I will not go quietly.

The stairs end at a hallway floored in rich, dark wood and lined with sconces. To the left end of the hall are grand double doors of carved wood. To the right, a white single-width door and in the middle, a narrow brushed-metal door with a keypad lock.

I'm led to the white one on the right.

The front guard steps out of the way, indicating I should walk into what looks like a living room with an open kitchen separated by a bar and stools. It's plain but clean and well kept, with large windows and a few pieces of nicely made furniture in squared-off edges and flat, inoffensive colors. The woods are warm, and one wall is exposed brick. The paintings are generic and abstract. There are no photos.

No one lives here.

A woman rises from the sofa—older than I am, with long yellow hair pulled back into a chignon, her face an indifferent mix of features that make her plain in a way that isn't unattractive, just nonspecific.

Why am I disappointed it's not Dario waiting with his cruelty and heat? Is it the challenge I crave? The potential? The sheer vertical drop into the unknown whenever I'm in his presence?

She stands and nods in my direction. The door closes behind me.

I do not move. I can't stop staring at her. She doesn't

look generic or nonspecific. She's a jogged memory of a woman standing in front of a black slate background.

"Miss Tamberi?" I whisper. "Is it you?"

When she smiles in a way that goes all the way up to her eyes, I know it's her. She takes my hands and steps away, holding them as if we're dancing. She's a little rounder and has more lines in her face, but she's my grammar school teacher, and the only reason she'd be here is to take me home.

"You can call me Dafne now," she says. "Should we get you cleaned up?"

"I'm sorry," I say, pulling my hands back. "I'd rather just leave now and clean up at home."

I'm bouncing on the balls of my feet at the thought of the familiar scent of my own soaps bubbling in the safety of my own bath.

"Oh, Sarah," she says, squeezing my shoulders. "You're not going back."

There has to be another sentence, so I wait for her to say, "You're going right to the church to get married," or, "The authorities want to see you, so you need to be cleaned up and coached in how to be silent."

But she adds nothing and tries to tug me across the room. I resist.

"Where then?"

She nods slightly, fluttering long lashes covered with powder-dusted mascara. "I know you remember me from... my Lord, how many years ago?" She makes herself laugh a little. But it's not funny. "I'm not teaching anymore."

"What are you doing?" I ask suspiciously—not just about her vocation. What exactly is she doing here?

"I work for Mr. Lucari." She says it with a lift at the end as if her job isn't disgusting. "Come. You'll feel better when you're clean."

My feet won't move. I'll never be clean after what's happened to me.

She tries to take my hand, but I snap it back. "Get away from me."

"Come," she says more firmly, with the voice of a teacher.

My school was in the basement of Precious Blood. It was the only school we knew, and you didn't disobey the teachers. Ever.

So, I come like a dog, following through the living room and past a paneled door. The bedroom's made up with a burgundy bedspread and drapes drawn over the huge windows. The oval wool rug is the only curve in the room. Everything is straight lines and right angles.

Dafne turns on the light in the suite's washroom, where she's drawn a bath. The mirror is already steamed up, and the air is thick with humidity. She leaves the bathroom door open.

"Let's get this gown off." Dafne tugs at the fabric.

I go limp. The silk falls away like meat off the bone. Wordlessly, she helps with the underwear, the shoes, every last scrap, until I'm as naked as Dario commanded the day before.

The open door has defogged the mirror, and I see my reflection. Even past the dust and dirt, I look frightened and frightening: shell-shocked and haunted, my eyes too big for my face, my cheeks and lips pale and chapped.

I'm led to lie in the steaming water, where she soaps and rinses my body.

"What's happening?" I whisper as she drops shampoo into my rat's nest of hair. She wouldn't clean me up for more torment even if she does work for a monster. Maybe I misunderstood her when she said I wasn't going home. "Is Daddy coming for me?"

"Not today," she says. "Lean forward."

She dumps on more shampoo and massages my scalp clean. My mother used to bathe me. But Grandma never did. I've never been so grateful for a rough touch.

"Please help me," I say when she's silent for too long. "I don't know what to do."

"Whatever Mr. Lucari says to do."

"No!" I shoot to standing in the tub, dripping soap bubbles and sheets of water. "He's a monster." The shampoo clouds my vision, and the sting in my eyes enrages me enough to raise my voice. "I don't want to listen to him. He's an outsider. He's a bad person. He made me naked in front of him, and I don't want to see him ever again."

"Sarah," Dafne says, pressing a towel to my burning eyes.

"No!" I snap the towel away and immediately see a change in the room—a splotch of darkness through the haze.

"Get a move on," Dario says from just inside the doorway. I cover myself with the towel, but it's too late. He's seen me naked again. "Or you'll do this dressed in foam." He pauses to look me up and down. "Which could be interesting for all concerned."

"That's enough!" Dafne barks, getting in his line of

sight. "Everyone will wait as long as it takes. And you..." Her arm shoots straight to direct him out. Though Dario doesn't seem frightened of the woman, he's somehow deferential. "You have no business walking in here like a pervert who can't reach his own dick to relieve himself."

He raises an eyebrow as if he's impressed with her command of language.

"I can reach," he says. "And my brain works. I don't need the visual stimulation."

"Out!" She pushes him—literally pushes him out.

He goes without a fight, giving me a glance in the split second before she slams the door behind him.

CHAPTER 9

SARAH

My grammar school teacher, who now somehow works for my kidnapper and is fluent with the word "dick," dresses me in cotton underwear, high-waisted pants, and a long-sleeved, button-front shirt fastened to the collar. I tuck it in myself.

"Good." She drops a pair of flats in front of me. "You look ready for anything."

I slide my feet into the shoes. "But what am I ready for, Miss Tamberi? Why won't you tell me?"

She holds my shoulders and leans down so her gaze can bridge the few inches of height between us.

"The goal," she says with low seriousness, "is for you to be safe."

"That's a lie." I reply with the same depth. "I was starved for days." Her eyes and hands disconnect from me, but I'm not done. "He made me drink fouled water. Naked. He pushed my face into his crotch until he came."

"The details aren't important." She's ashamed, and she should be.

But instead of addressing how I was treated, she leads me out of the suite and into the hall, where Gennaro and Vito wait. They take us to the double doors, which open at our approach.

We enter a waiting room done in the same smooth, modern woods and right into a conference room filled with men and women talking, standing, sitting, leaning on the windowsill until I enter—then all of them cut to silence.

Dario is at the center, and when he turns, the heat of his attention consumes me. I'm naked in the tub again, with a towel he sees right through.

I'm transfixed for a moment, but then there's movement behind him, and I become aware of the huge television screen. On it is the image of my father.

He doesn't look nearly as shaken by the last few days as I am. In fact, if you didn't know him, you might see a man entirely self-possessed. But I know better. The cuffs of his shirt aren't properly pressed because I'm not there to do them.

My heart hurts to see him this way. I want to throw myself against the screen's glass and crawl through its wires. I would do anything, I think, to be where he is—with my father and in safety.

"Daddy!" I cry like a child, not a woman of marriage age. "I'm here!"

He doesn't respond. The crowd cleaves itself as I rush to the screen.

"Please! I'm right here!"

I reach up to touch him, but Dario stops my hand.

"He can't hear you," he says. "He can't see you either."

"Why?" I can't work out the benefit of even having me in the room, then.

Dario turns crisply away from me and back to the screen. A woman in a business suit presses a button on the black plastic unit in the center of the table.

"Tamara," Dario says to the woman at the controls.

She's all business. Hair cut to the bottoms of her ears, parted in the middle, with a black clip holding it off each side of her face.

"Thirty seconds," she replies robotically.

"I can't see you," my father says, his eyes unfocused. So, we can see him, but the favor hasn't been returned. "You there? You got her?"

I stand electric with relief. I exist again.

The woman uses her fingers to count down from five, and Dario speaks.

"We have her. She's alive, more or less."

"Show me," Daddy demands.

"Oliver?" Dario says to a man at a laptop.

"Visual control over to you."

"And audio," Tamara adds.

Dario turns to Vito. "Get her out of camera range."

Vito pulls me back, and I disappear from the narrow attentions of the camera.

Then Dario addresses the rest of the room. "Everyone. Before we go visual."

People shuffle to the corners of the room. Dario holds up the back of his wrist, swipes the surface of his watch, then taps it. On the television, my father occupies a tiny corner window, and a new image fills the screen.

Me, naked before Dario, practically in his arms.

The camera angle leaves nothing but the wall behind us. No indication of our location.

Another tap and the video starts.

On screen, his lips brush my neck. My head tilts back in what looks like ecstasy. There is no sound, and I can only imagine the silence on my father's end as he watches me drop to my knees.

Even though I know what's coming, I'm shocked by it.

Dario takes me by the back of the head, undoes his fly, and forces me to suck his cock.

I know it's a pantomime.

Despite that, I am humiliated.

And despite both the farce and the disgrace, I'm tingling and wet with the memory of it.

I shouldn't be this aroused. Shame curdles in my stomach and spreads through my limbs. Until now, all of my miseries have been between me and my own weaknesses, but now my father is seeing me at my lowest. Even if I get to explain why it looks like it does and what I had been actually asking for, he will always have the image of me allowing a stranger to not only witness my nakedness, but also get his dick in my mouth.

Maybe it would be better if I had just refused, even if it meant my death.

Greenhouse Dario presses my head into him with both hands.

The video freezes there, and a little box with Dario inside appears in the corner. The greenhouse blinks back to my home, where my father stands, but now he has company.

Massimo, my darling brother and protector, has his arms crossed and his mouth set in a line of disgust. My father looks humiliated and furious, which doesn't surprise me. He saw what he saw.

"What do you want?" Massimo asks.

Dario smirks. He's been waiting for this moment.

"Leave New York. All of you. Go far away and hide. Take nothing with you. Leave it to me, and I won't chase you to the ends of the earth."

"You fucking nuts?" my father says, rigid and unyielding. "Our asses were here when StuyTown was a swamp. We built this entire city."

"Sure you did," Dario mutters.

"You're the one who needs to run and hide," my father continues, and that's when I realize I'd hoped he'd take the stupid deal to set me free, because he won't, and the death of that hope means I'm alone. I have to get out myself.

"Then I will take everything from you," Dario says. "Piece by piece. First, your daughter will be my wife."

"You will never," I vow to the back of his head.

"Hush!" Dafne hisses, grabbing my arm.

"Can someone shut her up?" he says flatly.

I'm yanked back by strong arms, and a hand covers my mouth from behind.

"I'm gonna use her body like a toy every night," he tells my father. "She'll swallow my cock and beg for more. She'll debase herself over and over again until I fuck the memory of you right out of her. She'll have my sons. Then I will take your money. Your assets. Your life."

I resist, squirming and kicking, but I'm easily restrained, like a leaf plucked from the wind.

On the screen, my father remains impassive. My brother is trying for the same reaction, but his cheeks are getting hot with anger.

"So," my father says, looking up as if trying to come up with the right words. "You think this kind of talk's gonna make me stupid?"

Every word cuts a cord. Between me and safety. Me and my people. Everything and everyone I didn't know I depended on. My muscles lose their will to fight.

For the first time since the conversation started, Dario looks at me, and I see something so incongruous in his expression that for half a second, I wonder if I misjudged him.

Regret.

"I thought it would make you human."

"Fuck you," Massimo bursts out. "We're not like you, Lucari."

"Tell her that."

A red light flashes at the top of the screen, and my father's expression opens. He can see the room.

"Daddy!" I cry with a rush forward, but men have me. "Emo!"

"Let her go," Dario says, tapping his watch again.

When whoever was holding me obeys, my own energy throws me forward.

"Goody," Massimo says coldly, leaning forward to inspect what he can see of me.

"You all right?" Daddy asks. "They hurt you?"

They're just questions. He's not panicked or desperate. Daddy's always been this way, and his level head is comforting, but it's not an invitation to lose my own cool.

Men are easy to read so we don't have to ask a lot of questions.

"I'm okay," I say with as steady a voice as I can manage. Daddy nods. They hear me. "I'm not harmed."

"This is your last chance, Peter," Dario says on audio.

"To what?" my father answers. "Tie up New York in a fucking bow for you? The entire city? This is what you want?"

"I want what any man wants." Dario shrugs. "An obedient wife with nice in-laws."

Massimo raises a single eyebrow and tilts his head. "You think marrying her makes you one of us? That isn't—"

Daddy interrupts his son. "Your marriages ain't shit to us. Wrong church. You're gonna get nothing. Outside weddings don't bring you in. They cast her out."

Dario smiles as if this is exactly what he expected. "You sure?"

"Am I sure of my own fucking dick?"

"Bye, Dad," Dario says, cutting the connection.

The image of my father, my home, my life, blinks to black.

They cast her out.

My father couldn't have been clearer. He's going to throw me away.

I've cried for the loss of my wedding and the ruin of my dress, for hunger and thirst and fear and pain. But this is the end of the world, and it's too overwhelming to shed tears about.

I'm orphaned. I'm a ghost. I am nothing more than one small, stupid girl.

I don't know how to feel, so I feel nothing as Dario barks

64

orders. The woman in the suit shuts her laptop and takes it away. Everyone files out but the man who stole me and the teacher who dressed me.

I don't know which direction I'm looking. Fear to my left. Sorrow to my right. Disappointment behind and rage before me. I stand on panic and under submission. But inside me, I feel nothing. I'm empty, waiting for the wind to blow something into my heart.

Dario turns to me at last. It's not the sharpness of his apathy that cuts through my directionless haze, but something closer to compassion pounding its way through the cool indifference.

I want to hit him. I want to throw flowerpots at his head, kick through his massive television screen. I want to tear the seams from his clothes and see how he likes it. If he feels the way he looks, why does he demand my suffering? Why does he insist on torturing me like this?

"What do you want?" I insist.

"An obedient wife."

"Liar."

That makes him pause, and I brace myself for a blow that doesn't come.

"Answering the wrong question truthfully doesn't make me a liar."

"What's the right question?"

His burst of laughter is shocking. "What's the difference? It's not going to change anything."

"I want to know!" My limbs are still, and my voice is even, but I feel like a toddler whining and stamping her feet. "Just to know. Tell me something I can believe."

He seems to understand this request and lifts his chin so he can look down at me from a higher perch.

"You'll believe it's about money. So believe that." He looks over my shoulder. "Get her ready."

Dafne puts her hand on my shoulder, and I spin on her. "You're a snake."

She gasps, and in my peripheral attention, I see Dario glance at her over my shoulder. I hurt her. Good. I've never hurt anyone before, but I've never been kidnapped before either.

"She's not your enemy," Dario says. "I am."

Now I focus on him because I may not know who my friends are right now, but the enemies are very clear.

His eyes are endless shadows, and I was raised to be strong enough to swim in dark waters.

"I'm not staying with you." My exhausted voice grabs for the last bits of conviction. "You don't understand what you're getting yourself into."

"Little *principessa*." He takes me by the chin like he did the day before, squeezing hard enough to hurt as he makes me look at him. "I know what I'm getting into when I marry you." He drops his hand. "Good thing you already have a wedding dress."

He walks to a door that goes deeper into the apartment, lays his hand on the knob, and stops.

"You could use a real fuck. It might be the only way to burst that bubble you live in."

He opens the door. The people he'd chased away are in the next room, talking softly and looking impatient. It's just Dafne and me when he closes it.

"Come." She puts her hand on my arm. "You've had a hard night."

"Traitor." I shake off her touch.

She walks away. Once she's out, they'll lock the doors. I won't be able to escape. I'll be alone with no one to love or hate.

All I can do is follow her and wait for my next chance to get out of here.

CHAPTER 10

SARAH

WHEN WE GET TO THE SUITE WHERE I WAS BATHED AND CHANGED, there's food out. I'm expecting more of the same—the ham or tuna fish sandwiches, soggy and salty in a plastic clamshell.

Instead, Dafne slices a long loaf of bread and sets it on the table with a fresh antipasto. I eat silently, deciding I don't speak to traitors on an empty stomach.

"When Dario becomes your husband," she says, puttering around the little kitchen, "you need to submit to him. Obey him completely."

"The marriage won't be correct." I assume she knows what she taught me herself. We came across an ocean as a Catholic people, but we left a long time ago. We're heretics, sure. But we're better, tighter, purer for it.

"The ceremony will be done properly," she assures me, but I don't believe her. She's a liar and a defector.

"You turned your back on us."

She emits a patient sigh I remember from school.

I push away my plate. I expect her to chide me the way Grandma always did—*we have no use for a wasteful or ungrateful woman*—but instead, Dario enters uninvited.

"All right, my bride-to-be," he says. "You've eaten? Good. Time for us to get married."

His cheeks are smooth-shaven, but he's still wearing his street clothes. No one would marry in that. He must be bluffing.

"No." I sit ramrod straight in my chair, defiant. If he wants me, he'll have to come get me.

I don't owe him obedience.

I don't owe him anything.

"Sarah," my teacher says.

"You can go, Dafne."

"But—"

"Get out." His tone has the crispness of absolute authority. I recognize it as one my father uses with difficult subordinates.

If you don't discipline them from time to time, Daddy told me once, *they forget what you're willing to do to get them to obey.*

Dafne leaves. I am alone with him.

What is he willing to do? And am I willing to endure it?

I make the calculation too late.

Dario crosses the room in three long strides and grabs me by the arm, yanking me up from the chair. I stand my ground, digging my heels against the hardwood floor. Then, giving in to my purest instincts, I use my free arm to punch him in the stomach.

For a moment, he looks more stunned than winded.

Fury overtakes me and I try for another punch, but he recovers and grabs my arm.

"I'll never marry you," I hiss, drawing close enough to spit in his face. "Never! Never."

It is the most interested in me—as a person—I've seen him look, like at last I have managed to surprise him enough to question if he's doing the right thing.

No matter, though. He isn't about to let me go. Instead, he backs me up against a wall, where he can hold me at a distance, too far for me to scratch or bite him.

"Get out of those pants and back into a dress," he orders.

"No."

"You think I won't make you?"

With a scream, I kick at him, hitting his shins, but I might as well kick a tree trunk.

In response, he drags me to the bedroom, where Dafne's hung up the bedraggled mess that was my wedding dress, a monument to the catastrophe of my life.

Dario tosses me on the bed, then throws the dress on top of me. I sit up and throw the dress to the floor.

"I will knock you unconscious if I have to." He surveys me, then the room, as if choosing a weapon to bludgeon me with.

"Do it." The challenge rumbles from an underused place in my chest. "It's better than being awake."

Dario isn't interested in what's better for me though, because he pushes me onto the bed, kneels over me, and with one hand in the center of my chest, pins me against the mattress while his other hand rips open my pants.

"This," he grunts, yanking them down, "is not working."

I struggle, kicking and biting, scratching at any skin I

can find, but it's no use; he is implacable, apparently impervious to pain, as he holds me down with his weight and uses my own against me to get my pants off, letting me twist until I'm facedown on the mattress, my feet are on the floor, and I'm naked below the waist.

He presses the back of my neck, and I'm sure he's going to use the vulnerability of my position to do whatever he wants.

"I don't want to take off your shirt," he snarls. "Because I'll rip it, and it's the only one I have for you. If I let you up, will you put it on? Or are you too much of a savage hellcat to dress yourself?"

I think of his hand skimming up under my shirt, touching my waist, my ribs, my breasts, even incidentally, and I can't bear the arousal my mind's been opened to.

So, I nod.

"Say it with words," he says. "Like you're civilized."

"Yes." I can barely speak with my lips smushed against the bedspread.

"Yes? Yes, what?"

"Yes, sir."

"Yes, what are you going to do?" His lips are so close to my ear I can feel the wetness of his determination.

"Dress myself."

"In what?"

"My wedding gown." A tear falls across my nose.

"Good girl."

He lets me up carefully, and I spin to sit up, putting my hands over the triangle between my legs.

"Modesty doesn't suit you." He drops into a leather chair by the window. It has gently curved teak arms and the high back of a throne. He slouches, knees spread wide at the angle of a dare.

"I can't escape," I say, wishing it wasn't true. "You don't have to watch me."

Once he's gone, I'll find a way out of here, and if I can't, I'll shred that dress from top to bottom. No dress, no wedding. No wedding, no Dario. He might kill me for messing up his plans, but it'll be worth it.

"Yes, Schiava, I do." One knee rocks back and forth like a metronome. "We don't have time for any of the delays or stall tactics you're thinking about. Dress yourself now, or dress yourself in the car after I strip you down and prance you down to the parking lot naked."

He would do it. All those men would see my body, and there's already been more humiliation than I can bear.

Standing, I turn my back to him, and in the mirror on the closet door, I can see him watching. My insides turn liquid under his attention, filling my clit like a balloon and soaking my folds in warm anticipation.

"I've seen beautiful women naked before," he says with exasperation. "I've even managed to not fuck a few." He pauses. "One, actually."

"I'm about to double your rate."

"Get on with it."

I take off my shirt, checking him in the mirror.

He's not gawking at me but looking out the window. Is it an effort to look away? Or does he have more self-control than the average man?

Why hasn't he raped me already? Just for fun? He wants to. I can tell that. What's holding him back?

I pull on the dress. The laces are still missing, so it's

loose, and I'm glad. The right fit would be an insult. I do up the buttons along the side, slipping them through loops I labored over, and turn back to him.

He stands.

"You make me a magnificent bride." He believes this. I am his ruined bride, magnificent in his eyes, and there's nothing I can do about it.

"I will not let you pollute me." I close my hands into fists. "You will never own me." I say it with all the authority of a sniper delivering a single lethal bullet.

He chuckles because though I may have ammunition, he's stolen all my weapons.

"Own you?" He chokes back laughter. "What would I do with you?" He holds his hands out to me, indicating the obvious. "You were raised in the middle of the biggest city in the world, but you were so sheltered you'd get lost going one-way across town. Your education was the bare minimum. You were taught to take care of a house but not how to pay for one. You're probably not even a useful lay."

I don't know why that last sentence hurts more than the others, but it hits deeper and harder, smacking away all my retorts. He takes out his phone and hands it to me.

"Call the cops. Tell them you're being held against your will."

I look at the glass with its colored squares covering a photo of a volcanic island between blue sea and sky, and I don't know what to do. I tap a square without looking too closely at it. Music plays before a singer enters with a moaning roar.

I put a spell on you...

"You're going to tell Screamin' Jay your problems?"

I tap wildly, but all that happens is the song changes. I push buttons. The screen goes black. There's a red button to make an emergency call.

I've got him now.

I tap it. Nothing happens. I tap again and again, but the phone just will not do anything. I stare at it, ready to cry, then I try the buttons on the side again. The screen goes black a second time.

Out of pity, he takes the phone back, staring at the screen pensively for a moment. "I'm not here to hurt you. Just do what I say."

"What if I don't?"

He tips his chin up, then closes his eyes, tilting his head to one side. When he straightens out, he's stone cold all over again. "'I'm not here to hurt you' doesn't mean I won't."

He crooks his elbow to me.

I'm supposed to take it.

I'm too tired to wrestle again, so I take his arm so I can fight another day.

I catch a glimpse of the two of us in a mirror as we exit: his strange, sliced-off ears and casual clothes, me in a dress that can no longer impress even the most dull-eyed. I carry that image out of the suite, feeding it to the fire burning quietly in my heart.

CHAPTER 11

SARAH

For the second time, I'm in the back of a limo on the way to my wedding. This time I'm blindfolded in a parking lot. He removes it when we're just another long black car on just another crowded street. He's facing me, legs spread, with a hungry gaze that makes me want to shrink into nothing.

The streets get more familiar with every minute. I can't lie to myself anymore. We're heading to Precious Blood. I don't know how he'll manage to marry me properly, but he will. Unless something happens to stop this, Dario Lucari will be my husband.

"I preferred the blindfold." I look out the window.

Outside the car, the world zips by, so big and frightening that generations of Colonia daughters were sheltered from it.

"I prefer to know what you're thinking," he says.

"I'm thinking the only thing between me and marrying you is a car door."

"Get through it if you can."

Denise was also ashamed on her wedding day. At sixteen, she had to marry Marco or be cast out as a whore. She did it to save her own life. I felt sorry for my childhood friend as she cried at the altar of Precious Blood, but girls got married at that age so often I figured it would be okay.

My compassion was tempered by the assumption that I was protected from the same disgrace. Grandma and Massimo would never allow me to be caught alone with a man in an empty basement the way Denise was.

"Here." Dario has a few Italian words with the driver and turns to me. "Are you going to behave?"

I don't know.

I've always behaved. That was the only way to make sure I had control. Denise didn't, and now she has four children when she only wanted two. Sometimes she cringes when she sits, or she stands very slowly for a woman of twenty. But she's also alive and married, and she lives inside the family with her children, whom she raises *our* way.

Can't say the same for Giselle Fiorentino, who had acid in her veins.

"I asked you a question," Dario rumbles like a man repeating himself with the last of his patience.

Giselle was fun. She and I broke into the sacristy above the Precious Blood school, and we ate communion wafers with jelly. We never got caught for that. Maybe the sin is still stuck to my soul and this is my punishment. Years later, for an infraction involving our pastor, Giselle was cast out. She could be dead for all I know.

But look where I am now. Goody two-shoes.

"I'll behave in a way that honors my family."

He leans forward until I can feel his breath and smell his

76

cologne. More than anything my five senses discern though, the psychic darkness inside him pushes against me and pins me in place.

"Your family has no honor," Dario says. "So that better mean you come as quietly as a woman beaten into a coma."

"I'm not afraid of you," I say as the car stops.

When I see the bolted gate and the boarded up stained glass, I realize where we are, and I clench in horror.

I don't know how, but we're going to be bound at Precious Blood.

The marriage will be done correctly. It will be unbreakable. Did Daddy and Massimo allow this? How could they?

"I'm not asking you to be afraid." The door behind him opens, and the sounds of the street enter. "I'm telling you to be quiet."

Dario gets out and holds his hand toward me. I'm supposed to let him help me. I don't want to, but my only other option is sitting in the back seat of his car with his driver behind the wheel.

If I stay, they'll drag me out.

If I kick and scream, I'll be drawing attention to Precious Blood and my family. After twenty-one years being told to do anything but that, I discard that strategy.

Church bells ring from another cathedral somewhere in the city. I sit straighter, wide-eyed after a deep breath.

It's Sunday morning! My church looks like any other neglected building in the city, but it has to be full of people —my people. Where else would everyone be?

Does this mean Daddy's approved of what's happening to me?

All I can do is get out, but I don't have to take Dario's

77

hand to do it, so I slide over the seat and get out without letting him touch me. It doesn't matter. Once I'm standing, he takes me by the elbow. I try to shake him off, but he won't let go.

"Don't." The word is low but pointed. "Just don't."

"It's Sunday. Church is full. You're walking into your death."

In the sunlight, with the cool autumn wind pushing his hair back, Dario's mask of shadows slips. His expression is so fleeting, and the mask snaps back on so quickly, I can tell myself it never happened, but it did.

Halfway between the car and the church, in a microsecond between hard and cold, I saw through him.

He's scared too.

A car horn blasts. The moment is broken. I turn away. The car is irrelevant, but I see a man in uniform approaching. A cop with a nightstick and a heavy belt under a low-hanging gut.

Colonia children are taught to never speak to the outside authorities...ever. But we are three steps to the end of my life, and this police officer could be the last chance I get to escape.

My mouth opens. What will I say?

The cop reaches up and touches his hat in greeting.

I decide to say the word "help."

But before I can take the breath, he looks at a place above and behind me, then speaks.

"Mr. Lucari." He keeps his stride and nods before offering four more words as he passes. "You're good to go."

And like that, my last escape route closes.

CHAPTER 12

DARIO

HER FAMILY DESTROYED OUR LIVES AND NEVER LOOKED BACK. NOT once. That's their strength and their weakness. They don't even know what they did, and I'm not going to tell them. I'm just going to make them watch me break their most valuable asset. Let them try to figure out why I'm dismantling their operation and taking what's theirs to drain them, bit by bit.

By the time I send Sarah away, I'll be standing on the ruins of their stagnant empire.

With a key Nico made for us, we enter Precious Blood through the basement door. No windows on either side and stained glass front and back, it's dark as shit.

The ceremony will be performed at gunpoint, which is about what I figured, on a Sunday, when they're all in one place—in front of me.

The bride wears dirty, wrinkled white and a mask of dead expression. I've seen it before. The open eyes that look inward because what's happening in the world is too horrible to watch, the slack jaw, the moment of awareness as we enter the church nave, as if she's waking into a bad dream.

When she cries, her eyes are huge.

I said I'd never force a woman. I'd never hurt or break one who wasn't already whole or play on trauma or weakness for my satisfaction. But she's different, and for the plan to work, she can't be just a woman. She has to represent the Colonia.

So, I decided a long time ago not to feel sorry for her. Colonia women aren't so innocent. They've died for their men, and their men are animals. They've committed the worst sins for the family, then the family imprisoned them by hanging those sins over their heads.

Adding the Cavallo men was a good idea. Vito and Gennaro are ferocious and well-trained when they relieve the congregants of their weapons. That's for the bride's protection. They'd just as happily shoot Sarah as continue to look at her.

Remo's the third of them and the youngest. He goes up and down the aisles as though he's passing around the collection plate, taking their weapons and handing them over to Connor the Aussie.

Nico's in the back. I see the curly top of his head, but we don't make eye contact.

It is not the day my bride fantasized about as she sewed the corset she has to press against herself. It's a day of violence and justice, one I have dreamed of since I was a boy and planned to the slightest detail.

What I didn't expect are my immediate regrets, especially with regards to the princess.

She's nothing more than a brain with useful information and a warm body with Colonia blood running through it. Once that body is bound to mine by their rules and laws, she'll turn into a key that unlocks a world I intend to pillage.

And also, she's beautiful, and tender, and sheltered—traits I despise because they're weak. All broken as easily as her loyalty.

Outside weddings don't bring you in. They cast her out.

On screen, with her in the room, her father made sure I knew that whatever I did to his daughter, the important thing was that I wouldn't get any of the privileges that came with the marriage. Already, her father's thrown her away. She's disposable to me, to her family, to her fiancé, to her own people.

I see myself in her because her reaction was to fight to belong. To my own disgust, I admire her loyalty.

She's at my feet now. After Vito shot a guy who tried to come after me, she fell to her knees with her dirty gown arraying itself around her. Her head's bowed, and her hands are folded in her lap.

"Please stop," Sarah begs. "I'm begging you. Don't hurt anyone else. I'll be good."

She's begging for her family and the people she calls friends. They'd sell her in a minute. There's no time to fight with her. She's going to sell herself to me to save lives.

Guilt is pointless. Wasteful. I should reserve it for anyone in the room but her.

I don't want to feel like this.

"Where's Father fucking Falcone?" I shout, scanning the congregation's shocked expressions.

Yeah. I know their priest's name. I know the Vatican didn't send him. He was raised to go to seminary in Rome so he could leave the Church and land at Precious Blood, where he'd spend four days a week in the confessional.

"Gennaro found him," Vito says from a stone archway to my left. "Coming right up."

These Cavallo guys are a machine. I'm going to send Santino DiLustro and his pain-in-the-ass wife a bouquet.

I see a movement to my right, and it takes me a split second to assess that it's a Colonia raising a weapon we missed. I whip my handgun out of its holster and shoot him, noticing his age (ancient) and dress (important person) between the time a flower of red blooms between his eyes and he falls.

My wife squeaks out a sob. I don't care. Let her cry.

"Anyone else want to die today?" I shout over the sound of her, looking around at a few dozen faces all wordlessly saying the same thing.

Yes, they say. *We all want to die.*

"Get your fucking hands off me!" a voice booms from the crowd.

Connor pushes Peter Colonia into the center aisle. He nearly trips on his uneven feet and brushes his jacket straight.

"Peter," I say. "Where's your boy?"

"What's it to you?"

"It's his sister's wedding."

Peter stands in the aisle with his arms crossed and his thick hips rocking back and forth. I'd shoot him right there if I didn't want him to see me degrade his daughter so badly.

"This isn't going to work." Sarah looks up at me as if I'm the one kneeling at her feet.

A howl rises from the dark tunnel Vito's guarding. It's a nauseating, cowardly sound that tells me the person who made it isn't as eager to die as the ones staring out from the shadows.

My guys drag in the priest. He's in his forties, shaking like a bitch.

The fucker ran when we showed up instead of protecting his church. Weak link. Probably not the weakest.

"Why isn't your brother here?" I ask Sarah.

"He doesn't come to church."

"How is that possible?"

"Massimo does what he wants. No one can control him."

She's just opened the possibility that there are dynamics at play I haven't prepared for, and I'm going to learn them right here, in enemy territory.

"Stand!" I growl, pulling her up by the excess fabric at the back of her dress.

She's dead weight, but her legs hold her, and after a moment, she pridefully tilts her chin upward like the fucking queen of the ball.

I don't have time to admire this shit.

The priest is pushed to the altar.

"You ready to do a wedding, asshole?" I say to the priest, then I look at Peter Colonia, who's still standing in the center of the aisle.

"I cannot," the priest says through pursed, prayerful lips. "Please, sir. I cannot. It is a death warrant."

He's resigned, as if he really can't and I may as well ask him to take out his own liver and cook it with onions.

I put my gun to the priest's head. He actually seems grateful for death.

"Peter. Tell him to do it." I look at Peter. "Or did you decide to start packing?"

It was never about getting all these scumbags out of New York. It was about asking for something they'd never give willingly—then taking it.

He rocks his hips so hard he goes from toe to heel and folds his hands in front of him as if he's cupping his balls before unleashing their power.

"Daddy?" Sarah calls to him, surprising me.

"Zip it," her father shuts her up before he nods at the priest. "Go ahead."

He's giving the weasel permission to proceed.

"I don't want to marry him," she squeaks. It's as if she didn't live with these people long enough to know none of them—not even her own father—give a shit what she wants.

I'll add her faith to the list of things I'll admire later.

"You'll do what you're told." Peter crosses his arms.

I've got firsthand experience with asshole fathers, and this guy's a new breed of the same. I don't even need Massimo.

"That's real brave, Peter." I say it as if he's the one I look up to, not his little princess. "I'll get you a father-of-the-year trophy."

He says nothing.

I take Sarah's limp hand. "When I'm done fucking your daughter."

My future wife's breath hitches as if she hit a speed bump at seventy miles per hour, but her father is unmoved.

"Let's go," I bark at the priest, taking a ring from my pocket. It's a cheap pawn-shop find I picked up in Sugar Hill yesterday. Gold with diamond chips in a six-pointed star or flower or maybe a snowflake. Whatever.

I take her left wrist and hold it out. Her fingers are balled in a fist. I start to forcibly open her hand. But before I can even do that, her father's voice echoes in the church.

"Open your hand."

She does it. Just like that. All her fortitude crumbles. It should be disgusting and pathetic. But it isn't. It's enraging and heartening because her utter obedience is what I need, and that pisses me off.

"No more fighting, Sarah," Peter says. "Do what you're told."

She holds out her left hand, palm down, fingers bent at the first knuckle. I push the ring where it goes, then lock my right fingers to hers, pushing my knuckles into her webs, making a flat surface between us.

"I don't have the knife," Father Falcone whimpers.

"Of course you don't, mate." Connor hands him a silver blade, two inches long. "No worries."

"Daddy, please." Her voice is tiny but still sounds loud in the stone room.

Her father says nothing, and that's even louder.

Without batting an eyelash, he just consigned his daughter to die the way my mother did, and I'm so angry I'm ready to blast this whole place to rubble, but I can't. That's how mistakes happen.

The coward priest mutters some made-up shit in Italian

that no pope ever approved. He lays the blade on our linked hands, adding pressure to cut us together, curving the edge across the tops of our fingers and creating a cut that'll make a scar unique to my wife and me. The lines will only connect when I hold her hand like this.

Neither of us even flinch when he cuts. Blood drips between us, adding to the dark staining on the stone where the crimson bond of marriage has been cut for centuries.

This part—the corporeal part—is done.

"There it is," I say to my wife.

"There it is," she replies in a tone that's much older and wiser than I thought she was capable of, her deep eyes steady and calm for all the pain she's experiencing. It's as if the ceremony opened the skin that held her innocence inside. Now it's been cleared out, and all that's left is a woman who forgets as little as she forgives.

Strange what a ceremony will do.

"Her body's mine." I address Peter while looking at her. We need barely a minute to make sure the way out is clear. "What should I do with it first?"

"You think dragging her in here and getting cut makes you one of us? I already told you. It don't work like that."

"Doesn't it?" I push Sarah to her knees.

I do it to throw him, but Peter's merciless, indifferent mask doesn't slip. He'd make everyone's life a lot easier if he'd just submit. He's going on a longer, harder journey to the exact same ultimate destination.

It's his choice, not mine. I don't care who among his people suffers; it's just twisted to have him confirm that he doesn't either.

"We got your name," Peter says. "We know your business. You got a lot going on for being such a little shit. I'm gonna take it all."

"Are you?" I yank Sarah's hair. Her lips part. "I'm gonna fuck your daughter's face right in your church."

My dick reacts to the suggestion, but Peter Colonia is unflappable. At this point, I don't know who I'm trying to shock besides myself.

"Fine." He agrees as if I'd just threatened to shampoo his carpets.

My dick turns to melted butter, and I fist my wife's hair so tightly her cool expression scrunches in pain. I want to shout at her. *Your people know nothing of love or family. Your own father's going to throw you to a wolf because he only loves power.*

But it isn't my job to tell her any of that. She can figure it out for herself, or not.

"Dario," Sarah says softly. Comforting. An opening into a negotiation I'm losing.

My name from her lips snaps me.

"Are we clear or not?" I yell to any of my men who are bothering to listen. The echoes peel the power away from the doubt. I sound terrified.

"Clear!" Gennaro calls.

"Nice doing business with you." I wave to Peter before shouting, "Let's move!"

I grab my new wife by the back of the dress again. She won't get off her knees, and fuck if I'm going to carry her.

"Get up." I squeeze her jaw in a vise. "Follow me or I'll snap your neck."

"Make me."

"So, this is how it's going to be?"

I throw her over my shoulder and run out the side opposite of the one we came in. She's mine now, and her pitiful screams won't save her from her new husband or her old family.

CHAPTER 13

SARAH

My wedding dress was meant to be bloodied when the cut was made, but as the wounds in my fingers stop bleeding and begin the process of scarring, the red streaks on white silk offend me.

This blood was supposed to be the sign of a bond that strengthened all of us. I was supposed to marry Sergio to expand our influence into new territories. It was already a dangerous marriage, but Massimo said we needed to branch out. He said Daddy knew I could handle it.

Daddy must think I can handle this too, but I can't help wishing that he'd found a way to keep me from marrying this animal.

We're in a different car than the one we escaped in. That one had a driver and barely stopped as we got in. We got out on 21st and into an old, empty Chevy Dario wordlessly ditched on 49th Street in favor of a Honda with tinted glass. He put me in the front seat as if he knew I wouldn't run and headed across town in a zigzag.

CD REISS

I never heard the doors lock. Could have missed it, or this could be my last chance to get away from him. I try to see trust in his angled profile. His jaw seems harder and squarer than before. I don't know why.

Then I do.

"You shaved." I touch the door handle. If I pull it, I'll find out if he locked it, and then what? I'm still married to him.

"So?" He glances in my direction, and I have to turn away.

Dario stops to let a businessman cross in the middle of the block. The pedestrian waves thanks, and Dario waves back. That guy's probably thinking, *What a decent guy*, tagging this encounter as one of the few with kindness he'll confront today.

"I've only ever seen you with a mess on your face." I'm insulting someone who could kill me, but my filters are shut down. "Badly kept. Like you don't care. So, why not today?"

If I open the door and roll out, screaming my head off, it could wipe the smile right off Mr. Suit's face. Show him decency is more than a right of way.

"I wanted to look nice," he says.

In my shock, I pause, and he presses a button to lock the doors. He doesn't have to. I can think of running all I want, but I won't. I can't. More than the sun setting over New Jersey and rising over the Atlantic, or the permanence of my Colonia blood, I am bound to this man. I can't escape him any more than I can escape myself.

DARIO PULLS the car into a parking lot dug under an unremarkable brown brick building—the first time I've seen it from the outside. I try to memorize everything. The keycard reader. The yellow-and-black arm that lifted, hitched, then lifted smoothly again to let us through. The exit signs. The yellow arrows. The numbers at the head of each spot. Lines of fluorescent lights set at regular intervals buzz overhead. One flickers as if it's trying to stay bright and failing.

Dario drives around a corner to a metal wall, then uses a fingerprint pad to get it to slide open. I memorize the signage and the lamps with the caged bulbs bolted to the brick walls on each side of the private elevator. Men stand under their brash light, waiting for the happy couple.

"Hey." He snaps his fingers in front of my face. "*Principessa*." He puts the car into reverse and throws his arm behind the seats to look behind him.

"Yes." I'm still in the fugue between escape and acceptance.

"I don't want to carry you upstairs." He backs into the space.

"They'll come for me," I say. "He said you could have me, but they'll come for me."

"Of course they will." His flippancy as he backs into the space is enraging. "You know too much about them."

"I don't know anything."

"You know more than you think."

The men standing in front of the elevator come forward. Dario stops them with a raised hand.

"You aren't my true husband," I lie to him and myself. The marriage has, technically, been properly performed. He

91

does own my body now. He might decide to take his pleasure from it at any moment, and there is nothing I can do to resist.

"The State of New York agrees." He puts the car into park and faces me. "But everyone who matters rubber-stamped this. I still expect obedience. Those are your rules."

"I will never love you." I clutch the door handle, but I don't have the strength to pull it.

"You think I did this for love?"

"You have my body and my obedience, but that's it."

He laughs, and the sound cuts me. "That's adorable."

"Set me free!" I'm twisted in my seat in a mirror of his posture.

He turns off the engine, leaving his left wrist draped over the wheel.

"Don't you ever ask me for that again." He's so handsome it hurts, and for a second, I wish he was one of us and we could be caught in a closet together. "Face front and put your hands in your lap."

I'm supposed to say no to an outsider, and I'm supposed to do what my husband tells me.

I'm not used to deciding between two equally vital and equally risky choices.

He waits, scanning my face as if he can see what I'm weighing. He rubs the smooth skin of his chin with fingers that bear the lines of his blood-caked marriage wound.

The pull of my upbringing claims victory over my distaste. I face front and fold my hands over my red-streaked skirt, covering my matching wounds. I pull my chin up and away from the sight.

"What do you think's gonna happen if I free you? Your

people don't want you. You going to get a job? Doing what? You're qualified to scrub a toilet, but you wouldn't know how to collect a salary for it. You could be a street hooker, except you can only fuck the one guy who's not paying. You'd starve to death inside a week."

"I'll take my chances." My voice is thick with the knowledge that he's right. A woman with nothing to negotiate has no chances to take.

"Do they even let you watch television?" he presses. "Have you read a book written in the last hundred years? Maybe give you a sense of what's out there in the world?"

His intensity fills the car. It's airless. I feel as if we've driven over a cliff and we're midway between the fall and the earth.

"I know what goes on better than you think." His words are cruel and hard, but his tone is unexpectedly temperate. "I'm not some weakling looking for a woman to tell me what to do. I don't need some bossy bitch laying down rules and telling me what's what. But you're literally useless."

One of the men by the elevator lights a cigarette. In the flame, I recognize Vito.

"Then let me go." I put my hand over Dario's. I don't expect him to think I'm touching him in affection—just sincerity. Seriousness. I want to convey that he's right, and if he'd just see me as human, he'd free me.

But when skin hits skin, something else happens—a vibration in my spine that shakes loose a warm fluid gushing between my legs. He moves his thumb to return the caress, and my brain goes utterly blank with unwelcome desire.

"I'm never letting them have you." His gentle edge tries

93

to convince me. "Never. Your father committed a crime against *me*, and he's going to pay for it with your life. They'll have to kill me first. In the end, you'll thank me."

No. I won't ever thank him, and he's out of his mind to think so. I take my hand away. Enough of this.

"I'll never forgive you."

His eyes widen a fraction of a millimeter. One lid twitches. I've triggered his anger. He can't have expected my compassion. Not after all he's done.

"Your mouth stays shut until I want to fuck it." He opens his door. The dome light goes on. We're reflected in the windshield, pale and translucent as ghosts.

"You're my husband." I submit to the truth of it. He might as well have lured me into a dark basement and ruined me. I almost wish it was that simple because the thought of his hard body on me turns solid resistance into molten surrender. "You're entitled to take what you want."

The words I think will pacify him actually enrage him further, and another shock of heat runs down my spine. He's even sexier when he's angry.

"You know nothing about what I'm entitled to."

Inside those words is enough ignorance to populate a city. My ignorance.

I cannot fathom the depths of what I don't know.

Now I am a student, waiting to be fed knowledge that's been denied me. The knowledge I don't have is a new source of shame without clear boundaries.

Before he can say another word, I jerk up the door handle. It opens as if it was unlocked this entire time. I get out, stepping onto the solid concrete but holding onto the car as if it's shaking under me.

TAKE ME

Strong hands help me stand.

"You all right?" Vito asks, cigarette bobbing with every word.

"I'm fine, thank you."

Dario gets out of the car and flicks his hand in my direction. "Get her out of my sight."

He walks to the door, flanked by two of the older men in suits.

"Let's go." Vito's not unkind, but he's not going to avoid hurting me if he has to, so I follow, tattered, alone, in a marriage that is as real as the ground under me.

CHAPTER 14

SARAH

WEARING A DISGUSTING DRESS AND FILTHY SHOES, I'M MARCHED back up to the suite no one lives in. Vito locks the door behind me.

On the counter that separates the kitchen from the living area, I find another sandwich in a plastic clamshell and a small bag of potato chips. Next to that is a pile of clothes with the tags pressed against plastic wrappers. Nightgown. Underwear. Jeans and a T-shirt shaped like a beige rectangle with two smaller rectangles for sleeves. A first aid kit.

While I was being married off to a monster, someone thought of everything.

I take a shower and put on the nightgown, then bandage my cut fingers that will define me as Dario's wife. I eat my wedding feast alone, looking down at the city full of people living their normal lives: hailing cabs, going to offices, falling in and out of love. I have always pitied the people in New York; they run headlong through a constantly changing world. My world never changed. Things were going to be the same forever.

Except nothing is the same.

The windows are as old as the building. Double-hung wood. If I press my forehead to the glass, I can see the street. How long would it take to fall from here to the sidewalk? Maybe I'll count on the way down and the answer will die with me.

The choice is too much of a game. I need to consciously refuse or accept this option, so I get my fingers under the frame and push up.

The old window opens about eight inches. I bend down to feel the outside on my face. The chill in the air threatens an early winter. The wind carries the rumble of busses and the wail of faraway car alarms.

I have to find a way to exist up here, in this world, because Dario's right about one thing. I don't know how to exist down there.

I close the window, shutting out the noise. Not my world. This carpet, this shelf, these drawers, these cabinets —these are mine.

When I see the ream of printer paper, I gasp out loud. Five hundred clean, bright pages waiting for me. Riches beyond compare. Like a woman searching for her soul, I open drawers, rummaging through the full ones and touching the backs of the empty ones, coming up with four stubby pencils and three ballpoint pens. I sit at the table and mar the pages with drawings, blind to time passing. I am not hungry or thirsty. There's no world outside the window or the other side of the door. It's just me and the lines.

This line is mine.

So is this one.

I draw the angles of the view out the window.

This is safe. I can draw this. Grandma won't—

She won't beat me because she can't get to me here.

No part of the world is closed to me.

A woman cries out. I freeze.

The cry is followed by rhythmic gasps, the grunts of a man, and the squeak of bedsprings.

At home, the walls of our apartment are thin. I hear the neighbors fight and bathe, eat and talk. In my early teens, I heard them make love with my ears to the plaster and my hand over the crotch of my underwear to make sure I wasn't being burned by a real fire.

Denise told me what I was hearing. The thought terrified and excited me.

Kneeling on the living room couch with my ear to the wall, I locate the source of the sounds. A slap. A giggle. A grunt so hard she can't have a stitch of air left in her lungs.

Dario has the space on the other end of the hall. Does he own every square foot in between? Is he the one grunting? Is my husband spending our wedding night with someone else? Who serves as my proxy? Is she experiencing pain or pleasure? Does she love him? Who could ever love that man?

Sliding my hand past the drawstring in my waistband, I find I'm gushing into my underpants. Two fingers probe deep, stretching the firm edges of membrane. It feels good, satisfying, right.

The creaks on the other side of the wall intensify. She cries out. No words. Just a vowel. More sensation rushes between my legs than I thought possible.

Digging deeper, the heel of my hand rubs against the hard nub at the front of my wetness.

That's the source of this feeling. I press against it, deep and hard, as the man in the other room says, "Give it to me."

My entire body tightens. My mind goes black. Lightning strikes along the length of my spine.

Then it hurts, and I'm bent over the couch, gasping from the physical release and split second of forgetting.

The couple on the other side of the wall is done. My body won't take another second of touching. But my mind races with desire.

This is what it means to be his wife.

It isn't about keeping the home and cooking the meals. It's slapping flesh and wet breathing. It's bending and twisting and moaning.

Sitting at the little table by the window, I turn angles into curves and draw the things I was never allowed.

THE NEXT MORNING, I'm woken by the snap of blinds being raised and a blast of sun. A man's voice cuts through my sleep fog.

"Let's go."

I blink hard. It's Gennaro.

"Boss wants you in ten." He's making every effort to not look at me. "Said to bring you naked with piss dripping down your leg if I have to but not a second late."

"Okay." I rub my eyes. "I won't make you pull me off the toilet."

"Good. Thanks." He doesn't leave.

"Did he say to watch?"

"No! No. I... ah... The sooner you're outta the washroom, the better." He jerks his thumb toward the living room. "We'll wait inside."

"Okay."

When I come out, they're waiting by the little table. Vito's looking over my stack of drawings, trying to covertly spread them out. A line-drawn, unshaded hand grabs a breast drawn soft with the side of the pencil, indenting the flesh with dark-shaded shadows.

I'm fully dressed, but I feel naked. My cheeks burn with humiliation.

Vito isn't my grandmother. He's not going to beat me with a wooden spoon. But I'm ashamed. I should have stuck to skylines and imagined flowers.

"Am I in trouble?" I ask, embarrassed that he's seen the naked bodies inside my head.

"No, no, I just... I don't know nothing about art... but..."

He drifts off, and I think, *Yes. I am in trouble.*

"They're really good," Gennaro finishes.

I gently take the stack, pile them neatly, and put them back on the table facedown. "Thanks."

He brushes back the few hairs he has left. He said they're good, but what he didn't say is that they've embarrassed him. I put the papers in a drawer built in under the window.

"We'd better go," Vito says. "Don't wanna keep him waiting."

We most certainly do not.

The men walk me across the hall, through the double doors, past the giant TV where I saw my father refuse to help me, and into the adjoining office, where Dario stands at the window with his arms crossed. He seems as immovable as the buildings below, as rooted in the earth and as extended to the sky.

He looks at his watch as if he's hoping I'm late. His jacket fits his slim waist and broad shoulders as if every suit in the world was made for his body, and I wonder if he's more or less feral without it.

My glance brushes across the flatly cut tops of his ears, a reminder that he has a history and it's made him capable of violence.

"Thank you, gentlemen." He turns away from the window, no less a part of the landscape with his face visible.

Behind me, the door snaps closed.

We are alone. I have never been more terrified.

CHAPTER 15

SARAH

"Good morning." Dario indicates an open door that leads
to another room. "I had breakfast set up. Have you eaten?"

"Not yet."

I let him guide me into the lush dining room, where
trays of bacon, eggs, and fruit sit on a dark wood table. He
holds out a chair for me, then he takes the one diagonal,
putting the cloth napkin on his lap. The fingers of his right
hand are bandaged—as are the fingers of my left.

"How are you?" he asks.

"Fine. And you? Are you all right?"

"Why wouldn't I be?" He leans forward in a way that's
not as threatening as it is curious, then takes the serving
spoons.

"I doubt that's how you imagined your wedding would
go when you were a boy."

"Maybe I was hoping for something more romantic?"

This is our most civil exchange so far. *Maybe this won't be such a bad marriage*, I think, only to stifle hope under the weight of reality. This will never be a happy union.

"Maybe not." I accept the eggs he puts on my plate, resisting the gravitational pull of his eyes. "Maybe when you were a boy, you planned to give your wife a glass of water with dirt in it."

"When I was a boy"—he adds a strip of bacon—"I didn't imagine a wedding at all. Or a wife."

"Of course, you were always this way. You never needed a woman."

"There are women I need. None of them need to be my wife."

"Except me."

"You can blame your father for that. I do."

I don't blame my father for any of Dario's actions, and I never will, but I'm curious how far this man will go for revenge. Whatever he blames my father for, was it a petty slight? Or monumental?

"What did he do to you?"

He looks right at me, taking stock of who I am and what I want. For a moment, I think he's going to tell me whatever the story is. Instead, he puts his attention back on breakfast.

"I'm not answering questions."

"This will be a short conversation."

He takes a forkful of breakfast to hide his smirk, then sips his coffee. "What would you be doing if you were at home right now?"

I've never known a man to take interest in a woman's routines. To men, the skills of women are easy. They aren't learned. They just happen like magic.

But he's not making light conversation. My silly routine may help his plan, whatever it is.

I eat and consider my options.

I don't really have any.

He's my *husband*. I have to obey. And confronted with the reality of him, I find I can neither remain silent nor muster the creativity to lie.

"Daddy likes boiled eggs and toast in the morning."

"Do you eat with your father?"

"If he's home, he eats breakfast and lunch in his office, and we eat in the kitchen."

"Who's *we*?" Dario asks.

"Me. Grandma." I avoid mentioning the names of the men who eat with my father in his office or the women who show up to work in my kitchen, which is the biggest. I'm not supposed to say names. My husband is still an outsider. "Then we clean up."

I shrug and bite the end off the bacon. The salt floods my mouth, making me realize how hungry I am. I inhale the rest of the bacon and start on the eggs.

Dario lets me get through half my plate, but he is not a patient man. "Go on."

"Today is Monday," I add around a mouthful of toast. "So, we're out of bread. Dough has to be kneaded. It needs to rise. Grandma usually helps chop the pork for lard bread. It's easier if we all work together, and I have the biggest kitchen, so..." Another shrug.

"'We' is the women?" He leans back, looking more interested than I gave him credit for.

"Yes. They take the dough home to bake."

"What do you do when you're done?"

"I'm never done cooking on Mondays."

"Tuesdays. Tell me about Tuesdays."

Is he going to make me go through the entire week?

"I get it now." I push away my plate. "You're not curious because you want to get to know me. You want to know my routines so you can figure out my father's."

He laughs and pushes away his own plate. "On Tuesday at 10:20, your father arrives at the Precious Blood rectory, where he runs his business. You and Denise—your best friend, who you hired to help to get her out of the house— bring him lunch at 12:30, and he eats it there. At 2:10, he reads the *New York Post* on the shitter."

"What's your point?" Now I'm the impatient one because the things he knows are terrifying.

"I can tell you where he'll be to the minute." He puts his elbows on the table. "I'm asking about *you*."

"You don't know?"

"I know where you are. Not what you're doing."

I swallow hard. How long has he been watching our every move? What else does he know?

"I've been preparing for my wedding to Sergio mostly. Getting the dress ready. The table arrangements. The food. It's been a lot, and it all went to waste. The apartment's been a wreck. I haven't cleaned my father's office in almost a week."

"You clean his office?"

"Just the one in the apartment. Do you want me to clean your office as well?"

"Do you ever look at his papers?" He taps a bandaged finger on the table. Is he trying to see if I'm honest?

"Why would I do that?"

105

"Curiosity is human nature, and your father has lots of secrets."

He's not interested in my days in the apartment Grandma and I shared with my father, basking in its sunlit simplicity and the feel of voices vibrating the wooden door against my ear.

"I don't snoop." I skirt the truth.

"You emphasized the word 'snoop.'" Dario has barely moved, but I can feel the focus of his intensity change.

"Did I?"

"You did."

"Should I say it again with less emphasis?"

"No. You've already told me where the lie is. You 'don't snoop.' What do you do instead?"

Dario is my husband. That single fact has changed everything between us. I can withhold the truth, but I cannot lie.

"I don't snoop. I... hear things."

He tries not to smile. He succeeds at keeping a straight face but not in hiding the effort. "You're a naughty little girl, aren't you?"

"No. I'm not."

Another smirk teases the corner of his mouth.

"And what does a wife do besides cook and clean her husband's office?" he asks.

"Raise children."

"How do you think children are made?"

How dare he ask this question. It's insulting.

"The same way..." Grandma Marta told me, but I cannot repeat it. It's impossible. "What you were doing last night. On the other side of that wall. Over my

106

couch. I heard... you and someone else. That's what
you do."

He pauses. I don't know what he's thinking exactly, but
he's looking inward as if unraveling a puzzle. He clears his
throat and takes a long blink. When he opens his eyes, the
puzzle is solved.

"You were listening," he finally says.

"I heard..." I stop. Dario seems to know me better than
myself. Evasion is a waste of energy. "Yes. I listened."

"Were you turned on?"

I try to take a deep breath, but my lungs won't cooper-
ate. All I can manage is a quick nod of assent.

"You're a naughty little slut, aren't you?" He leans
forward. "Did you put your fingers on your cunt?"

The filth of the word makes me recoil, but it also has its
own heat.

I nod again, but he slams his hand on the table so hard
the silverware rattles.

"Speak! Did you touch your wet cunt?"

In shame, I look at a crumb on the tablecloth. I press my
finger down on it and brush it off over the plate it missed
the first time. I am naughty. I've thought of myself as perfect
and well behaved because I never expected to get caught
with my hand in my underwear.

"Yes."

"Don't look down," he says. "You're my wife. Hold your
head high."

I do as he asks and level my gaze on his. A wall-sized
window stretches behind him, capturing the cloudy sky in a
gray rectangle.

"Hold my head high about what? You shaming me? You

think that's a distraction from what you did? Last night, on our wedding night, I had to do it myself because you were giving yourself to another woman."

"Is that what you heard?"

"Yes. I heard it all. Her moans. You grunting like an animal. Then you told her to—"

Give it to me.

He comes behind me and puts a hand on each of my shoulders, thumbs touching skin, sparking an electrical current of desire I thought I'd quenched forever.

"Describe what you think was happening."

"Sex."

"Was she on her hands and knees? On her back with her legs open? Was I teasing her with my cock or buried deep?"

I can barely breathe. No one has ever talked about what goes on with that part of the body except to say babies came from it, husbands will use it, and it's a wife's job to let them.

"Did I come inside her or on her tits? Maybe I wasn't in her cunt. Maybe I was fucking her ass." He leans down to whisper in my ear, "Do you want me to fuck you like that?"

"Stop. Please."

Between rage and shame and the urgency between my legs, I can't bear another moment.

"I asked you a question, Schiava."

"What does that mean? That word you call me?"

"Rule number one." He squeezes my shoulders hard enough to hurt. "No questions. Only answers. Do you understand?"

"Yes."

"Look at me when you say it." He takes my chin and points it upward.

I've spent the meal looking at either my plate or my husband, and now I'm forced to notice the mirror on the wall opposite. I'm wrung out, sallow, tight-pinched, and thin-lipped while the clean musk of him fills my nostrils.

"You look like shit." His reflection is shadowy and beautiful. And honest.

"Are you pretending to care?" I break rule number one. "Or just trying to insult me?"

"Just making an observation." He slides his hand from under my chin back to my shoulder.

"Then observe that it's your fault I look like this."

That comes out harder than I intend, but it still feels right. He's my husband. He's owed obedience but not necessarily courtesy.

"It is." He takes the weight from my shoulders when he steps back. "Stand up."

I do as I'm told. He removes my chair and yanks away the tablecloth. Food splatters. Dishes clatter and spin. When I try to turn to face him, he stops me and bends me over the table, facedown, looking at a streak of butter. One hand grabs my hips and pulls toward him. With the other hand, he pushes my cheek into the slippery smear.

"Now." He leans on my face. I can see the clouds over the city and a few building tops rising from the bottom. "You already broke rule number one." He bends close. "So, we're going to talk about consequences."

I say nothing.

"Rule number one is: no questions." I feel the rod of his erection against my bottom. He's going to take me now. I hate him, and yet... I want him to rip away my virginity. "You asked two. You're getting a spanking for each."

"What?"

"That's a third," he hisses, then takes his weight off my face and moves away. "I own you. Everything in your brain is mine. Every word out of your lips. Your body is mine, and I will make you hurt... gladly, daughter of Peter Colonia. I will hurt the fuck out of you and everyone you love."

He can. Just like any other husband, he can do whatever he wants. But I don't have to be some meek little kitten.

I look over my shoulder to ask why he wants to hurt us, but I rephrase. "I don't want you to hurt my family."

With one hand, he pulls my pants down to just above my knees, leaving my underwear. I'm grateful for the thin cotton that stands as a flimsy barrier between us so that at least he won't be able to see everything.

"I married you to hurt them. Open your legs."

"I can't. The waistband."

"Rule number two..." He kicks open my feet, stretching the elastic between my knees. "When I tell you to do something, you obey."

He puts his hand on the damp crotch of my underpants and presses them down flat, making circles.

"Let me up!"

I try to stand, but he only increases his hold on me, pushing me into the table edge with his hips. His dick feels thicker and harder than I ever thought possible. He pushes the underwear aside and slides his fingers deep inside me.

"Oh, God." I gasp.

"You're wet."

"Take me if you want to."

"You don't tell me what to do." He undoes his belt. The

buckle clinks. "That should be an easy corollary to number two."

I press my lips together and look out the window at the flat gray sky.

There's a whoosh as he pulls the leather from the loops, and that's when I realize he's not going to pull out his dick and use it. He's just removing the belt.

Oh my God.

He's going to do a full correction.

The only thing that keeps me from sinking into despair is the fact that I've been through this before.

CHAPTER 16

SARAH

"RULE NUMBER THREE..." DARIO LANDS A HOT, STINGING *THWACK* against my bottom. I gasp in shock. "You tell me everything I want to know. Answer every question completely. Omissions and half-truths are as good as lies."

He lands a burning stripe across my bottom. I bite back a scream. I'm not supposed to scream when I'm hit.

"Four." The next one lands exactly where he's already hurt me. The pain is searing. "I am your husband. Your first loyalty is to me."

He pulls down the underwear. Now he will hit my ass without that thin buffer.

"Let me tell you what that means, my darling."

My darling? I look at him over my shoulder. He's observing my burning ass like a starving man at a buffet. He's looking right at my wet center. He wants to fuck me, and I can't do a thing to stop him.

Except I don't want to stop him. Not even a little.

When he touches my ass, the skin burns, but another part of me buzzes with bewildering lust.

"It means you will betray your family when I tell you to."

He pulls back his other hand, and an unbearable sting blossoms over my ass as the belt lands full force. My knees bend in surprise and an arousal that's so violent it hurts more than the whipping.

"Straighten up!" he barks.

I do it, parting my feet again. The waistbands stretch across my thighs. I can feel the throbbing low hang of my clitoris, full with warmth, turning violence into sex. When he lands the belt on my bare, already-sore ass, it's not the burning pain that brings more tears, but the knowledge that I am powerless, and at the same time, I have so much more strength that needs to be stripped away.

He pulls my ass up and forces my back down, and I'm shamefully pliable. He hits the tops of my thighs, where I don't expect it. I feel blood rushing there, hot and red. I brace for the searing leather. It falls where my ass meets my legs, and a trickle of fluid flows inside my thighs.

"Number five." I hear the belt drop. He uses both hands to grip my burning ass and spread me open. I am fully exposed to him. "This is mine." He taps my seam with the back of his hand, and the pleasure blossoms from the pain. "Mine to fuck. Mine to suck. It gets wet for me and only me." He rubs it, but this time, there's no underwear to blunt the sensation. "When I ask you about my property, you speak up."

"Yes."

"Did you make yourself come last night?"

"I think—"

CD REISS

At my unsurety, he flicks my clit with a fingernail, lighting me on fire. I know what he wants. "Tell me what it was like."

"It was like dropping a plate. Waiting for it to fall. When it hit the floor, it shattered. Then it was broken. Not a plate anymore."

"Very good." Dario slides a finger inside me, and my mouth opens with a silent groan of mindless pleasure. I almost explode but, by some grace, hold myself. "But it won't happen again. I own this cunt. I own its orgasms. Whenever you give one to yourself, you're stealing from me. Do you understand?"

"Yes."

"You're wet," he whispers. "I'd love to take you right now. Fuck you blind right here." He takes the finger out and replaces it with two. My knees bend and my toes curl. "You're so sexy like this. I'm tempted." He removes his fingers and uses them to circle the hard, wet knot at the seat of my pleasure. I try to hold back a groan but fail. "Do you wish I'd fuck you?"

Yes. Yes, I want him to fuck me, but I don't, and yet... I'm outside myself. Muddled. Not thinking it through to its logical conclusion. All I know is that yes is a betrayal and no is a lie.

Dario takes his hand off my pussy, leaving me with a throbbing ass and aching clit, too breathless to confirm or deny anything.

"Yes!" I cry. He puts his hand back.

"Do you want me to make you come, Schiava?"

I am married to this outsider, pussy wet, nipples hard, wishing he'd take my body and use it in ways I can't even

114

ask him to. And that's the point. I can't ask my husband for pleasure. I can only give without complaint.

"Yes."

I don't know how he might react to victory, but he simply says, "Good girl."

In three violent flicks of his fingertips, the plate hovers in midair. He pulls it, then circles the tip so gently he's barely touching it. The imaginary plate goes higher and higher.

"'Schiava' means 'slave.'" He yanks me back by the hair. "Because that's what you are. My hot little slave. Show me how you look when you beg for it."

No. I can't beg him. I hate him. But the pressure inside me has a mind of its own. His touch is only enough to make me want him more.

"Please."

"Please, what?"

"Please, I don't know what to ask for."

"Jesus." He gasps the prayer. "You're so innocent for a whore."

When he calls me that terrible name, something in me is called and breaks free, and his touch is suddenly enough. The plate drops to the floor, smashing in a satisfying spray of sharp edges and dust. I cry out as his fingers go harder, then softer, extending the release.

My knees go weak. I collapse, satiated and sore, my face pressed to the cool wood, breathing hard. With the rush of adrenaline leaving me, my ass hurts more than ever, and I know very well what it will feel like tomorrow.

"Good girl," Dario repeats, helping me stand and turning me to face him. "Pull up your pants."

I obey, sobbing with the power of the release and the humiliation of my need.

He takes out a handkerchief and dabs my tears away. This single act of tenderness is bigger than the city itself and deeper than the bedrock it's built on. I hate him for it, and I never want it to end. I take the handkerchief.

"Thank you." I can't believe I'm thanking him. I just exposed my ass so I could be whipped like an animal and called a slave and a whore, and I'm grateful. The most humiliating thing about it isn't even how sexually aroused a beating made me, but how I'm melting under his single moment of kindness.

"Now that you know the rules, I expect you to follow them."

I count them off in my head. One, two, three, four, five. I can remember them. No questions. Obedience. Truth. Loyalty. He owns the orgasms. I can even follow these rules... except for one.

"I know them," I say. "But I'll never obey rule four. I am Colonia. Always."

"You are." He touches my chin pensively. "And yet you bleed and cry just like the rest of us."

"I'll never be like you. You'd probably let your own mother die for a dime."

Like lightning, he takes me by the throat and pushes me against the wall. The hanging photos clatter.

"Don't." His clenched jaw is two inches from my face. "Don't you ever."

The manhandling is something a woman has to deal with. This is the way of it. And though I hate that I'm aroused by his hand on my throat, I love not being afraid.

His expression is pure fire, and I wonder if I push him, will he bend me over for the belt again? Will he just slap me? Or will he fuck me? Will he beat my body with his dick?

"Ever?" I choke out a rule-breaking question. I might as well beg him to break parts of me with parts of him.

He considers it. I feel the possibility welling from his shoulder to his arm in the change of grip—sense his change in posture is a way to throw me on the floor or rip my clothes off.

But he doesn't. There's an expression under his anger, and it's guilt.

His head whips to the side when the door opens again, and a woman walks into the room.

Dario takes his hand off me, and I have to hold myself against the table to keep from falling.

"I'm sorry." The woman's voice is small as a bird's and just as melodious. "You sent for me."

She's small and dark-haired with a plain white blouse and jeans that don't fit her particularly well. Her hands are folded in front of her, and her gaze is trained on the floor.

Dario's watch beeps. *One-two, one-two-three. One-two, one-two-three.* I wonder if it's the alarm that this woman was going to walk in the door. He shuts off the sound, but not before I see two letters on the screen.

NL

"Take care of my wife's ass," he barks, striding for the exit. "Get it ready in case I need it."

He leaves without another word, slamming the door.

CHAPTER 17

SARAH

THE WOMAN TWISTS HER HANDS TOGETHER AND LOOKS AT ME WITH quick eyes that dart as if I'm a wild animal she doesn't want to get too close to. When she speaks though, her voice is soft and friendly.

"My name is Oria," she says. "Shall I call you Sarah? Or Mrs.—?"

"Sarah's fine."

"You're safe here. We're not going to hurt you."

"The first thing is doubtful. The second is already a lie."

"He said to take care of your ass..." She waves at my body with a relaxing, shameless grace. "Are we talking internal or external?"

I take a moment to understand what she means.

"External."

I already feel a sort of kinship with her that I can't explain. If he hurt this girl—who can't be any younger than I am—I'd find a way to kill him.

"I have some nice lotions set up in your bathroom and a change of clothes."

I follow Oria out, across the empty hallway, and back to the suite's bathroom.

"Do you want to clean up first?" She opens the cabinet and pulls down tubes and soft containers with pumps at the top.

"Yes, actually. I do."

"Should I leave while you get undr—"

She stops when I pull the shirt and bra over my head in one movement. Showing my body to other women has never been hard for me, but my enflamed bottom will be visible when I take off the pants, and the shame of what I allowed... what I *liked*... turns my cheeks just as ruddy.

I turn on the shower while Oria keeps her attention on the products she's arranging on the counter.

"Body wash." She holds up a container and a clean washcloth.

As I take them, I see a red tube of lotion with gold script. *Narciso*. I unscrew the top and sniff it. Dried flowers and sweet, dark rum.

"That's for after," Oria says.

Denise asked me to rub this exact lotion on her bicep, where her husband had given her friction burns.

"Where did you get this?" I ask.

"This little place in SoHo." She shrugs. "Do you not like it?"

"It's fine." I hesitate to pull the pants off. "Can I do this part alone?"

"Sure." She smiles brightly. "I'll meet you in the bedroom, okay?"

119

She leaves me alone, clicking the bathroom door behind her.

It's that sound, after days of locks clicking to hold me in places I don't want to be, that finally makes me break down in tears. In the shower, I curl onto my knees and sob as hard as I can, expelling every bit of sadness, disappointment, and despair. The sound of the water falling masks my crying for what I betrayed so quickly for a man who hates me.

I'm exhausted, and I'm hurting, and I'm *married*, and the only thing I'm certain of is that my life will never be the one I was raised to live. Even if my father bursts in the door right now and rescues me, I'm ruined. I'm still a virgin, but there's a video of me kneeling naked in front of Dario.

Finishing the shower, I get out and wrap a towel around me, shivering as the water gets colder on my skin.

I wipe the fog from the mirror. The strip immediately mists over again, but for the first time since I sat at breakfast with my husband, I am totally awake and aware. I am clean and cold, and I know my enemy.

Dario wanted to fuck me—could have with or without my permission—but didn't.

This time. He will have me eventually, whether I want him to or not.

What then? Am I just used up? Finished? Rejected by the men of my tribe to serve a man who hates them?

Is there anything I can take back for myself?

One cunt hair pulls more weight than two oxen.

Grandma Marta used to mumble that after fighting with Daddy to get married again.

She'd know what to do.

What if I could see her again? If he's not afraid I'll escape, would Dario let me?

If I give him my virginity, he'll believe the Colonia won't take me back—and maybe they won't—but all I want is to see my family one more time.

I enter the bedroom wrapped in a towel and new purpose.

"You should lie on the bed," Oria says delicately. "Then you can take a nap."

"I'll stand." I drop the towel and put my elbows on the dark wood dresser, exposing my wounded ass to Oria.

In the mirror, her expression is simultaneously compassionate and businesslike, as if she has no interest in judging the ass she gently smooths the cream onto.

"Does he do this to you?" I ask. "What he did to me?"

"No." She keeps her attention on her work, making a project of silence before she adds, "Did you tell him to stop?"

"Where I'm from, you don't tell your husband to stop." I look forward again but bow my head so I don't have to look at my self-loathing or her lack of judgment in the mirror. "You take it unless you're weak and unworthy."

"But did you *want* him to stop?" she asks, kneeling to get to the backs of my thighs.

I hadn't wanted him to stop whipping me unless he was going to fuck me. That's a hurtful and true fact.

"He can be cruel." She saves me from a lie or an admission. "But he can also be kind."

I scoff because no matter what Dario does, I'll hate him.

Even when I let him fuck me—which I will—I'll hate him.

And if he lets me see my family, I'll hate him.

121

She's done with her ministrations, and I dress myself as she talks.

"I was scared of him too when I first met him." She snaps the lotion cap closed. "Well, to be fair, I was scared of all men. I'd never met one who didn't want to use me, and I didn't see why he would be any different."

"Did you fall in love with him?"

"No." Her serious face splits into a smile. "God, no." Then she turns serious. "He saved my life, and I'm grateful to him for it. He didn't have to. He barely knew me. But he saved me."

I can't imagine this version of Dario, someone kind or thoughtful or even basically human.

Is she pulling him by the cunt hairs? It seems impossible that such a small, melodic voice could make the sounds I heard through the wall on my wedding night, but I consider the ridiculousness of my twinge of jealousy and know it's more than possible.

If I want to go home for a visit, I'll have to let him grab me those hairs. Let him ruin me until I'm too broken to redeem.

"How did he save you?" I ask.

She pauses, looking at her hands lying palm up in her lap.

"My mother stayed home, and my father was an electrician," she says. "I had a sister and a brother, and we were fine until..." She chews on the memory.

"That's fine." I try to wave it away. "I don't want to pry."

"My dad got hurt in a broken elevator. His back, I think. He couldn't work. So, my mom didn't have any skills really, and we had no money, so one day a man came and said I

could help with living expenses even though I was thirteen."
She swallows, then says the next part so fast the words run
into each other. "He took me away to have sex with men,
and I didn't like it."

"Oria." I kneel in front of her chair and place my hand
over hers. To my surprise, she grasps back. "I'm so sorry."

"For a long time, I still had this hope I'd go home and my
dad would be better and things would be like they were. But
some of the girls with me were older, and they were broken.
So, I resisted. Not with my body, but my mind." Tears shine
in Oria's eyes, but they don't fall. She steels herself the way
she must have learned to all those years ago. "I was giving
up on myself, and Dario got me out."

Now she's burning with an evangelist's zeal, her face lit
with love for this man—her liberator and my captor.

She jumps out of her reverie when her watch beeps in
the same rhythm as Dario's did.

One-two, one-two-three. One-two, one-two-three.

Does her little screen say NL? I can't see.

"I have to go." She stands. "You'll be all right here?"

"I will." As if I have a choice.

She practically backs out of the room. The lock clicks
behind her.

I'm alone with my knowledge.

Dario's soft somewhere. If I can find that place, I'll use it
to see my family.

CHAPTER 18

DARIO

BETWEEN THE OPEN CABINET DOORS, THE SCREEN HOVERS ABOVE the dark conference room. I have to calm down before Nico appears on it.

I didn't leave my mother to die. I know that. Nico knows it. God knows it.

But Sarah said it, and I was thirteen again. Exposed. Unsafe. Left in the bitter cold with nothing but grief. I wanted to die with her, but couldn't leave Nico alone, so I fought myself, then I fought the world.

I battled the cops with their heavy black belts slotted with bullets, and the Feds with their barbed threats and lethal education. The hustlers and the psychotics. Rival bosses who hurt me at first, but eventually I brought them all to heel.

When Nico was old enough to take care of himself, the only thing that kept me alive was the Colonia. Vengeance is my breath. It's my fire. It animates me when the air in my lungs might be my last and the puddle of blood in the gutter is my own.

I have room for loyalty but not devotion.

I can offer sustenance but not guidance.

I am capable of affection but not love.

Hatred of the Colonia occupies the biggest rooms in my heart, and it's bolted to the floor. Only retribution can remove the anchors, and only justice will haul away the dead weight.

Sarah's been the means of my revenge since I learned her name.

I'll take her body when I have her soul.

When she said yes, I'd intended to use what I owned, but something dark sparkled in her—an unexpected shadowy fire.

Her body isn't enough. I want her mind and soul. Her every desire. I shall own her very will.

All of it.

Nico blinks onto the screen. "What's the word, thunderbird?"

"You tell me."

"They're searching for you like you got the last cookie ever baked. They'll drag her back whole or in pieces. Makes no difference to them. But you? They're gonna put a circular saw where your legs meet, you know what I'm saying?"

"They have to find me first."

"That's what I'm worried about."

"It's my job to worry. Just keep your head down and your eyes open."

Nico is as invested in revenge as I am, but the biggest part of his job is kindness, as it should be.

"Did you find out about the shipments?" I ask.

"I got a list of them." He slides a loose page from his notebook and holds it in front of his camera. "Some are gonna be just tax-free cheese and fish, but one of them will bury these people."

"You're a magician." I list the dates on a legal pad with four bandaged fingers. No matter what happens with Sarah, my marriage to her is cut into my skin from the barbaric wedding ritual.

"I am. I so fucking am."

"It's going to scare the shit out of them when we're waiting there."

"Speaking of scary shit, how's the old ball and chain?"

I don't have to tell him I plan to make her love me before I turn on her. He's known too many Colonia women to abide that kind of cruelty.

"She snoops." I put down the pen, finished.

"Really?" Now he's leaning forward.

"Cleans Daddy's office. Then she tells me she 'hears things' through the door sometimes."

"And?" He rips the paper into tiny pieces.

I lean back with my palms up. "I need time to squeeze her."

"How much time do you think you have before she's gone, like *poof?*" He puts his fingertips together and splays them to illustrate how quickly my wife will be out of my reach. "The war's gonna start for real, and it'll be a pain in the ass for her to tell you shit even if she wants to."

"I'll get it out of her."

"How?"

Behind me, the door opens quickly and clicks closed.

"Hey," Oria says.

"How is she?" I ask.

"Fuck you, man." She sits next to me. "You didn't have to do her like that."

Oria is two people. We accepted this long ago. In front of strangers, she's timid and docile, but once she knows you're not going to hurt her, you get what you get.

"Hey, baby." Nico leans into his camera.

"Hey." Oria's voice is soft and thick, and in one syllable, a guy can tell exactly how she feels.

"I miss you so much." Nico has forgotten why he's even in the damn room. "It hurts right here." He jabs a thumb into his sternum.

"Poor boo," Oria says.

"I am a poor, poor boo."

"Did you cut your hair?" she coos. "It looks hot."

"Just a trim. But you? My God, you're stunning."

"Before I puke," I interrupt. "First off, Oria, I did have to do her like that. She expects a correction. It's what she's used to."

"Ouch." Nico cringes. "You did a correction?"

"Don't make it about her." Oria looks me up and down. "You left that room with a battering ram in your pants."

Nico puts a fist over his mouth when he laughs as if it's going to be loud enough to blow his cover.

"You should worry when I don't."

"But why?" Nico says. "You have a completely subservient wife. They respond to direct orders and direct questions. Every man's dream."

"You can shove that," Oria says.

"Almost every man." Nico turns back to me.

"She'll do what I tell her."

"Nah," Oria says, surly. "You got a long road with that one. She's a princess. She's had it too good."

"She's a spoiled brat," I agree. "Useless in the real world. But she's gold. She knows things she doesn't even know she knows. We'll be using her information for years if we play her right. But if we rush—if she's still loyal to them when we send her off—this whole thing was a waste of time."

"You gave her the stick," Oria says. "Now the carrot."

Immediately, my senses become flooded with Sarah. I can see the red of her ass and hear the moans from her lips. The tang of her sex bites my nostrils.

"Second thing." I sit up straighter. "We stopped the conjugal visits months ago." I catch them glancing at each other. "She heard you two through the wall. What the fuck were you thinking, Nico? Are you trying to blow it all coming here? You trying to bring them to the door?"

"It was my fault." Oria jumps in front of trouble.

"No—" Nico starts to take the blame.

"I miss him."

"It was me."

"Shut the fuck up. Both of you," I say. "You want to die? Have at it. But I have three floors of people working for me. When you fuck around, show up here—"

"I wasn't followed."

"You endanger everything." I slam the desk with my palm. "Every fucking person in this building." I stand before I have to hear excuses or apologies. "Armistice Night." I address Nico with the mention of the annual meeting of the heads of every mob family in the country. "Find out who they're sending."

"The Colonia don't go to that." Nico knots his brow. "At least not before last year, when he trotted out his daughter like a—"

"Thanks," I say as if he's agreed. "You're the best. Stay safe over there, will you? And don't come back here until it's safe. Those people are savages."

"No shit," Nico and Oria say at the same time.

I cut the call and lean back in my chair. It squeaks again.

"He's not safe." Oria points at the screen where Nico's face was.

"It's at least as safe as bringing him back here for a fuck."

"You need to get him out of there, now."

Oria wants to execute the entire plan all at once, and all I can think about is taking my time. I have never wanted to ruin a woman as slowly as I want to ruin the Colonia *principessa*.

I take thee, Schiava, to have and to destroy, from this day forward.

"He comes back when we're ready." I leave.

Sarah will obey me. I know how to use the sugar of the carrot and the pain of the stick. She'll be so beautiful when she breaks. Her mind, her body, her will—I'm going to relish every moment I spend crushing her before I send her away.

CHAPTER 19

SARAH

THE FREEDOM TO DRAW WHAT I WANT IS AN OBSESSION. FOR TWO days, I can't stop putting every picture in my head onto paper. I show Oria the drawing of her chin, how it changes shape when she smiles, and the veins in Grandma's hand as I remember them. She brings me two more reams of paper and a scrambled handful of pencils and erasers. I am in heaven. I don't need references. It's all been in my head, and now that the egg is cracked, I'm whisking up omelettes.

There was the orchid in Daddy's office once...

And the way the spirali pasta curves...

The comb marks in Gennaro's hair...

The perfect creases of Dafne's shirt...

The scars on my fingers...

The three lines of muscle in Dario's jaw when he tightens it...

Also the swirls of his ears, cut off at the top...

Lips thick and wide...

Dafne interrupts me, walking right in as she always does

when she comes to make sure I'm eating and sleeping, but she gives me a heart attack in the meantime. I hide the papers as though a Colonia teacher caught me committing a crime.

"I've been knocking." She puts a load of pink shopping bags on the table.

"Sorry." I gather the pages, then pluck the crumpled white balls that have bloomed on the floor.

Dafne leans forward with prying fingers and tries to peek at my drawings, the imagined nudes, the still lifes, and the detailed corners of a man I hate blown up to a full page —but I snatch the pile away. I still despise her. She is a traitor.

"I was thinking," she says. "Since you're here and I'm a teacher, maybe I can help you finish your education."

"I finished with flying colors."

"According to the Colonia. Yes. But to the outside?"

The very idea that outsiders are better at anything, including educating children, is absurd. I won't even talk about it.

"Did you bring me something?" I glance at the bags.

"I picked out most of it." Dafne pushes them toward me. "I hope you approve."

I don't because I disapprove of her in every single way, but I unwrap them. Neutral-colored long skirts, two soft sweaters that match the bottoms. Socks. Underwear. The second bag contains a navy wool coat with a blue scarf, mittens, and cap that are the only things in an actual color.

"It's fine," I say.

"You should consider at least a little science." She picks up the third, smaller bag. There's a box on the bottom.

"Why?" I pull out the box.

"You like to cook. You can learn about heat on an atomic level. Why food changes when it's cooked. How nutrients work." She points at my drawings. "We can find a way to integrate art."

Dafne sounds more alive than I've ever heard her. She must miss teaching.

Denying her the pleasure of tutoring me will be fantastic... except that I'm trying to get Dario to trust me enough to see my family. He won't if I refuse the kindness of traitors. Agreeing costs me nothing, and she'll tell Dario.

"That will be fine." I undo the ribbon holding the box closed.

"Great! I... uhm..." Instead of finishing, she clears her throat as I lift the lid. "Mr. Lucari chose that."

"I'll be sure to burn it, then." I open it. A small envelope sits on top of tissue paper folded to hide its contents. I open it with a side-eye at Dafne, who looks as if she wants to crawl under the table.

Across the hall for dinner. 7 p.m. Wear this under your clothes.

—D

Dropping the note, I unfold the tissue paper to reveal black lace, buckles, straps, and bra cups. I lift a pair of black lace panties. The crotch is solid cotton with two snaps at the front and a slightly stiffer panel inside. I bend it, not sure what it's for, but it doesn't seem uncomfortable.

"I have to get a lesson plan together," Dafne interrupts my thoughts with hers. "Two days? We can start—"

"He wants me to be fuckable." I stuff the lingerie back into the box. "He thinks—" I don't say it.

He thinks they won't take me back if he ruins me.

He's right.

I expected this, and if I want to see my family again, I have to follow through.

THE LINGERIE IS SCRATCHY, but I wear it under the long taupe skirt and cream sweater. My door opens at a minute to seven. Vito and Gennaro wait in the hall.

"You look nice," Vito says.

"Shush, dipshit." Gennaro jabs him with his elbow. "Boss's wife."

"I said *nice*. What's wrong with nice?"

"Thank you," I say to Vito as we walk across the hall. "I appreciate the totally platonic compliment. I look like a vanilla ice cream cone in July."

Gennaro shrugs. "I like ice cream."

"Whoa, easy there." Vito acts deeply offended. "Boss's fucking wife."

"You're a fucking idiot." He opens the double doors and stretches his arm for me to enter. "Go on ahead. Right through."

He and Vito bicker on the other side, but otherwise, I'm alone in the cold little reception area.

I head for the room where my father watched a video of me on my knees before Dario. Depopulated, the room feels haunted. The black, spiderlike device with buttons sits in the center of the long wooden table surrounded by pushed-in chairs. A water jug and clean, upside-down glasses sit atop counters. Above them hang closed black cabinets. I tip one open.

Just boxes. I let it close. I don't belong here. I felt this way whenever I heard a snippet of my father's conversation that I wasn't supposed to, but this swell of excitement is bigger and a different shade of dangerous.

In the panic and real danger since my aborted wedding day, I've forgotten how much I like the thrill of stealing forbidden knowledge.

There's a stack of mail on a tray. I casually brush over the envelopes, then flick a finger to spread them into a fan. I know what junk mail looks like. I know what bills look like, but though these envelopes are plain and official looking, they aren't addressed to Dario Lucari. They're addressed to addresses. *The 1032 Lexington Ave. Corporation, 177 E. 70th Street Corporation,* and *326 E. 54th Street.* There's a postcard from a land of turquoise seas and white sand. "St. Eustatius" floats over a palm tree in yellow script. I look around, see no one, and flip over the card, laying it on top of the stack as if it had been that way.

Dearest Dario—
You should see the beautiful girls here... and they'd love to see you.
;)
All my love—Willa

The wink face is enclosed in a heart, but the handwriting is not a child's. I'd bet my body a grown woman wrote this, but no one's taking the wager.

Who are the beautiful girls? Daughters? Is Willa a lover?

The only one? Or one of many? Is she a pimp? A dealer? A partner in a criminal enterprise? Are the girls options to sell? To screw? Or is 'girl' code for something else entirely? In any case, the intimate tone of the card can't be dismissed. Is there perfume on it? The scent of adult hormones? Or is that just the aroma of the salty sea? I reach down to pick it up so I can press it to my nose but freeze when I hear soft shuffling footsteps on the other side of the second door to his apartment.

I'm snooping.

CHAPTER 20

SARAH

S<small>OMEHOW</small>, I <small>GET THE POSTCARD DOWN AND PICK UP THE PITCHER</small> before the door is fully open.

"This is empty." I rock it back and forth.

My husband wears trousers and a crisp white shirt. The sleeves are rolled up over tattooed forearms. He stands with his feet apart, taking up the entire doorframe as his eyes bore a hole in me.

He knows. He has to.

"Come in," he says after looking me up and down.

He gets out of the way, leaving me enough room to walk past him and catch a whiff of burned popcorn and a hint of a citrus cologne. The veins and tight skin of his forearms distort the script of his tattoo, but I can read it for the first time.

StuyTown

"I lived there." I point at the tattoo. "I was seven—"

Before I can finish, he picks my face up by the chin and

tilts it up to him. The tips of his hair are dark and slick as if he's just washed it, and his jaw and cheeks are shaved clean.

"You look hungry." He drops his hand, and I keep my chin up without its support. He leads me into the same room where he fed me breakfast and fingered me to orgasm.

A feast has been laid out for us—the kind of thing we should have eaten on my wedding night. A platter with two small roasted birds sits in the center of the table, their skin burnished gold; it's surrounded by tomato sauce and blond polenta swirled into peaks next to a white ramekin of jewel-bright vegetables. Places are set at the head and foot of the table, each with a glass of straw-colored wine.

Dario pulls out my chair. Same one as last time. "Sit."

I hesitate, remembering the merging of pleasure and pain the last time I sat there.

"Why am I wearing lingerie to dinner?" I stiffen as the words leave my mouth. I'm not supposed to ask questions, but he doesn't react with a punishment.

"Because I said so." He taps the back of the chair. "Now sit before I pick you up and sit you down myself."

Again, I hesitate, but dinner smells delicious, and I notice a basket with a napkin over it. I want bread, and if I have to sit first to get it, so be it. I tip my head down and slide into the seat as he pushes it forward, then he puts his hands on my shoulders.

"Take something," he says. "Eat."

"I should wait for you."

His fingers tighten, and I know that with his grip, he's demanding obedience, so I lift the linen. The loaf is half sliced and radiating wet warmth.

Dario reaches over, takes a slice, then butter and a knife, and puts them close to me.

"You're all set." His hands slip away. "I'll be right back."

I twist hard in my seat so I can see him disappear into the adjoining room. I straighten, face myself in the mirror over the sideboard, and eat the buttered bread.

He returns holding a shirt-box-sized object wrapped in white tissue paper. He puts it next to my plate and sits.

Chewing slowly, I try not to stare at the box. This is a gift, but why buy the good will of a woman he already owns?

"I'd ask you how your day was," I say. "But I'm not supposed to ask questions."

"Open it." He snaps open his napkin and lays it on his lap. "Or eat first. But stop ogling it like it's the only thing in the room."

He can't be jealous of a box. And yet he picks up his fork like a grumpy adolescent.

I unwrap the tissue paper to reveal a dark wooden box with a brass latch. The top is carved with a three-masted ship in the center of a frame of ropes. Sailors do nautical things in the corners. It's incredibly intricate with delicate inlays of shifting colors. I look up at him, and he nods, telling me it's all right to open it.

Slipping the latch free, I slowly lift the top. The inside is lined in red velvet with removable shelves and pockets, each filled with pencils, pastels, and chalk. There are three erasers, a rubbing stick, and a pair of scissors. It's an art set for someone whose work you don't know. It's everything and nothing. It's a nice try, and I appreciate it.

"Thank you." I close it. "It's lovely, but I don't know what it means."

"Yes, you do." He leans forward and serves me one of the birds. "Polenta?"

I nod, restructuring my question into a statement as he picks up his knife.

"I've never had this before."

"*Quaglie alla cacciatora*." The accent slides from his tongue. "Quail. Every time my mother made it with chicken, she talked about having it with quail. In the old country—as she told it—they breed like cats."

He was a child once. I can't imagine it.

The bird rolls when I push my fork to the top of it.

"Here." He reaches over to take my fork and knife.

"I have it."

He ignores me and turns my bird on its back. "The first couple of times I tried to cut this, it ended up in my lap. Hold the fork like this. Good. The knife cracks it open first." He does it for me. "Then you cut."

"Thank you." I take the utensils.

"Be careful of the little bones."

He's trying to please me, I realize. Actually trying. Probably because he thinks that if he keeps me happy, maybe I'll be more pliable. Or maybe this is that kindness Oria insisted he possesses?

I didn't believe her then, and I don't believe it now.

"Eat," he commands, and I obey. The meat is gamey, stringy, and layered with flavor. It's the best thing I've eaten in a while. Neither of us speak for a few bites.

"Dafne saw my drawings." I point toward the box. "That's how you knew."

"My wife's not going to spend her free time making pornography with a pencil stub."

"Those pictures weren't for you."

He pushes my wine glass an inch in my direction. I obey the wordless command, and the sweet bite loosens my tongue.

"I never had enough paper," I say. "The first drawing I remember making was in the margins of a book. I got my first correction that day."

Chewing, he looks up at me with possessive intensity, then turns back to his plate. "Go on."

"The second was a while later. On one of my mother's old hankies."

"Did you get a correction for ruining the linens?"

"My mother embroidered the drawing in. So, no. It was our secret."

"Glad to hear it." His nod is a reprieve for someone else. I wait for him to say who and why, but he doesn't say. "What did she embroider?"

"A snort."

"A what?"

"A red steam shovel." I shuffle food around my plate to find the perfect combination of flavors. "It's from a book she used to read to me. It's about a little baby bird who hatches while its mother is looking for food. The baby bird goes all over town asking dogs and cows and whatever if they're its mother. And all the animals are nonplussed at this lost baby bird."

I keep eating and, with a glance, make sure he's listening.

"None of them stop what they're doing and help or take

a minute to say, 'Listen, kid, you're a bird, so your mom's a bird. Look for a bird.' The bird asks an abandoned car, and it's so used to not being helped that when the car doesn't answer, it moves right on to a steam shovel... this huge monster which just snorts out a cloud of smoke, and the baby bird... well, just loses it. Throws a tantrum because it's all alone and no one's helping."

"He was probably hungry."

"Yeah." I eat around the last of the little bones. "I never thought of that."

"Drink something," Dario orders, and I obey with the wine.

"My mother told me the bird's screaming sounded like chirping... so the steam shovel hears it—or the guy inside it hears—and finally, the bird gets picked up by the shovel, which is terrifying, by the way, and put back in the nest where the mother's waiting with lunch." I take the last gulp of wine without being told and put down the glass. "And the world didn't start caring, but they lived happily ever after."

"Bravo." Dario claps slowly. He gives a satisfied nod and puts his napkin on the table. "Thank you for that moving story about being returned home by a monster."

His applause had seemed sincere, but it's soured by his tidy analysis.

"I didn't mean it like that," I say with my attention on my near-empty plate.

"You don't wish you had the same ending?" He taps his watch, then slides his finger across the glass.

Is this an opening to ask for what I want? I hadn't thought it would come this quickly.

"I'd like to see the nest again."

"The monster may dangle you over it." He taps the watch twice. "But not if you're in any condition to stay."

A warmth gathers between my legs. I'm not sure what's causing it. Not his forearms leaning on the edge of the table with the tattoo of StuyTown scripted over the East Side skyline. Not the way the buildings ripple over his muscles or the way his right fist softly knocks the tabletop.

The fork drops from my fingers. The skin of my thighs tingles. I'm panting like a sprinter in a heat.

"You're a good girl, Schiava." He sips wine nonchalantly. "I thought you might defy me, but you didn't. Good for you."

"It's the underwear," I say, remembering the stiff panel in the crotch.

"You like it?"

"No." I clutch my napkin and look away from him.

"Let me see if I can fix that." He taps his watch again. What started as a gently rising warmth I couldn't place turns into a definite vibration. "Better?"

My body betrays me, melting into the chair, eyes closing, lips parting. In the time it takes for him to get up and stand behind me, I'm soaking wet.

"Lift your arms." He pulls my sweater up and off. "Good girl."

He slides the chair back and away from the table, then comes around to face me in my bra, his arms crossed, observing the way I fall apart under the relentless pleasure.

"Why are you doing this?" My hips pump slightly but rhythmically. I can barely keep my mind on anything but the need to have an orgasm.

"That's a question." He taps his watch again, and the

142

vibrations slow. I squeak because sitting on this precipice is torture.

"You don't have to make this effort. You can just take what you want."

"I know." He leans down and pulls my skirt over my waist, exposing the tops of the stockings and the straps holding them up. "But I know you want to see your family. How can I send you to them raped when I can send you a whore?"

CHAPTER 21

SARAH

"Here's the deal." He speaks casually while I squirm with the vibrations of the underwear. "I'll let you see them, but only after I've taken you, and I won't take what you won't offer."

"You want to make it easy for me to offer. Okay. Yes. I want both. Please."

There's no downside here. I get everything but the ability to stay where I belong.

"Open your legs."

I barely have to be told. It feels so good to spread my knees far apart, on opposite sides of the chair, but it's not enough for him. He stands between my legs and pushes them wider. I look up at him.

"I want to see my family," I say as he strokes my face. "I'll do whatever I have to. I won't fight."

He smirks. "Don't get me wrong. I love a good fight." He shoves three fingers in my mouth. With his other hand, he undoes his pants. "But when I free your mouth, you're going to say yes or no. Not maybe. Not 'you can do what you want.' Yes or no."

Once I say yes, there's no going back. Yes means I give up my value to this man right now, but no leaves me isolated and alone.

"Yes or no." He removes his fingers from my mouth to take out his penis. "You going to suck this?"

It's huge, hard, deep red with a jewel of moisture at the tip.

"Yes or no?" he presses. "Which is it?"

"Yes."

He doesn't even smile.

"You ever suck cock?"

"No."

He takes his hand off his dick and hovers a finger over his watch.

Tap it. Turn it up. Let me come.

He taps it twice, then with thumb and fingers wet with my saliva, he grabs under my jaw.

"What do you want?" he asks.

"To suck your cock." The words are filthy in my mouth, but the underwear is pulsing with a beat that drives shame into silence.

"Suck it, then." He presses my cheeks hard, forcing my mouth open, and guides his dick in, sliding it against my tongue. He grabs my hair, controlling my head. "Go *ahh*, little Schiava. Open your throat."

I don't know what he means by opening my throat, but I go *ahh* and he shoves his cock down my throat. I want to heave.

"Hold it," he says. "Keep your mind on your cunt."

145

The rage of arousal between my legs feels like an indefinite plateau, but the gagging stops, and he pulls out. I gasp for air, spit dripping down my chin as he looks down at me.

"Good girl." He taps and swipes his watch. The vibrations get harder and faster.

"Oh, God," I gasp and arch my back.

He fists the hair on top of my head to draw me to him. "Again."

I open my mouth wide, and he uses it. When he pushes hard, I let go of the breath shaped like an *ahh* and take him.

"You're going to look so pretty when I make you come." He pushes my face to him. "You want to come?"

I can't speak. All I can do is look up thinking, *I do. I do want to come, please.*

He pulls out. "I didn't hear you. Yes or no."

"Yes," I cry. "Yes, I want to come."

"There's only one way you're coming tonight. Broken with blood on my cock."

"Yes!"

Dario kidnapped me, starved me, humiliated me in front of my family and community. He's made me cry harder than any man ever has in my life. And right now, all I want is his dick to break everything between my legs.

"Fuck whatever you want," I say. "But don't forget we made a deal."

He yanks me up, controlling my whole body weight with one arm, and throws me faceup over the table. Silverware clatters. My elbow tips the gravy boat. A wine glass rocks on its base but finds its center. Laying my hands on the table, I try to straighten, but he pushes me down by the sternum.

"Say the deal."

"I let you take me. Make it so they won't have me back. Then I can see them."

"Do you want me to fuck you or not?"

"Yes."

"What if I said no family? You'll never see them again."

"You wouldn't go back on it."

"Do you still want me to fuck you?"

I'm ready for it. I don't care if I'm soiled by an outsider forever. I don't care if I walk the streets, banished from home for the rest of my life. I'm not in my right mind. I want him to rip me apart with his dick.

And then he takes his hands off me. Is he going to leave me spread-eagled on this table, begging?

"I can keep you on the edge for days." He's about to tap his watch. He might turn the vibrations down. He might turn them up. He might make my underpants buzz "The Star-Spangled Banner."

"Please," I say through gritted teeth, eyes pressed shut. "Please just do it."

"Do what?"

I open my eyes. "You don't know?"

"Say it." He lifts my knees until I'm splayed in front of him. It's a shameful, humiliating position, but for some reason, I am not ashamed. "Say you don't care if I let you see your brother and grandmother."

"I don't."

"Say you want it even without the toy against your cunt. Say my cock is the only thing that will satisfy you."

The words can come out of my mouth, but will they be true? Is his cock the only thing I want?

I can't lie to my husband.

"I don't know," I say. "You can believe me or not, but I don't know how it'll feel when you take my virginity. It might satisfy this... feeling you're making me feel, but it could make it all worse. You're the only one who can. I'm begging you to fuck me. Please show me everything a woman knows. Please."

He must believe me because he answers by unsnapping the stiff crotch of my underwear, leaving me suddenly unstimulated, swollen, exposed to his view. With his thumbs, he spreads me apart, inspecting me. It's as degrading as having my feet in the *staffa*. Worse because he's not proving my virginity. He's checking the place he's going to defile, now using one hand to open my lips.

"I've never seen a clit this hard." He flicks it. I buck. He holds me still and does it three times, back and forth, until I cry out. "Sweet little thing." With his cock in his fist, he rubs the head along my seam. "You're mine."

With that, he jams into me so hard the breath is knocked from my lungs.

"Mine." He thrusts forward, stretching me, ripping me apart.

I let out a short scream, and he holds still.

"Don't stop," I say.

"It's going to hurt."

"I want it to."

"Good." He takes me by the knees, spreads them, and pushes them back. The third thrust buries him and finds a new kind of pain deep inside me. "How does that feel?"

"Like you're tearing me apart."

"Yes." He pulls out a little, then slams into me again, but this time, the pain is tinged with a knot of what the buzzing promised. "This is what I'm going to do to the Colonia." He drives into me over and over. "Destroy them. Ruin them. Find their weakness and rip them to shreds." He slips his thumb between us and circles my clit. This is everything I ever needed. "They'll take it. Just like you."

He pushes in, rubbing me until I'm a blind woman running down halls, looking for a room I've never seen before, feeling the walls for it, shaking locked knobs.

"Come for me," he says from behind one of the doors. I open it, and pleasure bursts out.

WHEN ORIA COMES IN, I'm drawing Dario's hair curling over the hard-edge of his ear. And his jaw. The line the back of his neck makes.

She puts a bag of groceries on the table and looks over my shoulder. I let her see the picture, thinking nothing of it. He's my husband. I can draw the parts of him I'm curious about.

But she takes a deep breath and sets her lips into a hard line.

"Is it not good?" I hold the picture at arm's length to assess it critically. "I think the angle of the—"

"It's good." She unloads apples for the bowl at the center of the table. "I can tell exactly what it is." An expression of irritation flashes across her face and disappears. "Dafne says she's coming for a lesson before lunch. These are in case you get hungry during."

She balls the bag in her fist.

"Oria. Are you okay?"

"Yes."

"I want you to tell me. I don't want you to be timid or scared around me."

She takes that as an insult, as if she wasn't a little mouse when I met her, but softens her reaction, clearing her throat to remove the last vestiges of negativity. I'm reminded of how Grandma trained me to do exactly the same thing. An offended woman isn't appealing. Anger is ugly.

"Not many people have seen Dario from that angle." Her voice is soft and low. She takes the page by the corner and slides it closer.

"Not many people marry him."

"True," she says. "True."

The second acknowledgement of truth seems more profound than the first.

"Oria?"

"I have to go. I'll be around if you need me."

She leaves with her secrets unspoken.

CHAPTER 22

DARIO

Now, she is mine.

Utterly, completely mine.

Down below, the city is Tuesday-night quiet. Brake lights crawl up and down the FDR like a glowing eel burrowing into clay.

There was never any point in fucking her if she didn't want me to. That would have been too easy. Also, not my thing. Completely unarousing. Guys who get off on pounding a girl while she cries and begs them to stop usually end up on the wrong side of my fist.

I could have gone a lifetime without getting my dick in her because I only needed to marry her. I didn't need to own her. But Sarah Colonia, under me, pleading to get fucked blind? That's the degradation I fantasized about while I laid plans to steal her.

She fucking turned it all around though. I wanted to uncover a latent whore who begged for my cock, but that's not what happened. What I ended up with was a virgin ready to become a woman, and if she had to go through me to do it, that was fine with her.

Dishonor and degradation slid right off her and landed on me.

The shower is ice cold, thickening my blood to a standstill and sending alarms through my nerve endings. I wash her off my hands and dick, remove the sweat I shed for her from my skin and hair, and step out of the shower.

When I fucked her, I wanted to consume her, to rewrite her body's knowledge of itself and drain every bit of Colonia blood.

"Fuckers!" I slam the water off as if the lever is Peter Colonia himself and I want to break it. I towel off as if he's stuck to my skin. I need this hatred. I do not need Sarah.

An alarm behind a mirrored cabinet door double-beeps. I open it. There aren't any cameras in my apartment, but the front door's on a sensor, and sure enough, it's been opened.

I reach under the vanity, feeling around for the gun I've duct-taped to the side of the sink, and rip it off. Check it.

God, please let it be Peter Colonia coming for his daughter.

Shutting off the bathroom light, I slip into the bedroom, then down a hall, where I find whoever it is walking toward me in the dark. They stop when I put the gun to their head.

"Jesus!" Oria says. "Paranoid much?"

I punch the light switch. "Don't you knock?"

"I knocked." She covers her eyes because I'm naked. "Can you put that thing away?"

Assuming she's talking about the gun, I lower it.

"What are you doing here?"

"I'm not making an appointment. I need to talk to you right now."

"So talk."

"Can you put some clothes on?"

"I can. You want to watch?"

"Thanks. No. I'll wait in the living room." She turns and walks away.

When I'm dressed and ready, she's not in the living room but the kitchen, clicking a coffee pod into the machine.

"Do you want one?" she asks.

"Pass."

"You're sending her to Saint E's, right?" The coffee machine gurgles and steams behind her as she looks me up and down with her arms crossed, reading me like a job hunter scanning the classifieds.

"Have I ever laid out another plan?"

The coffee beeps, and she takes the cup in her palms.

"You weren't supposed to fuck her. Are you starting to care about her? Because if you are..." She shakes her head to complete the thought.

"Why do you care?"

"What do you mean why do I care? I've been in this with you guys from the beginning and Nico—"

"Wait," I interrupt. "You misunderstood me. When I said, 'Why do you care?' I meant, 'How is it your business?'"

"Fine."

She storms away but stops at the door.

"Have you ever tried to wake up from a good dream?" she asks. "Like, scream yourself out of it?"

"I don't sleep that much."

"When you woke me up, I was living in a nightmare."

"I know."

"Sarah was living in a fine, happy dream. She thought she was living in the perfect little world."

"Your point?" I ask.

"She's not going to open her eyes one morning and say thank you. I'm not sure she'll ever wake up."

"Even a spoiled brat can wake up to reality."

"And what are you going to do to fill the space where her family was? We can't take it away and leave her empty. When you took it out of me, you filled me with revenge. You can't do that with her, and you can't fill that space with your dick."

She's wrong. I can fill it with my dick until my obsession with her fades.

But not before.

"What's your point?"

She tightens her jaw and crosses her arms. "Get Nico out of there. Bring him home."

"Not until they're crushed."

"That was not the deal!" She lowers her voice, but her tone remains barbed. "After the wedding, he was supposed to be out."

"If Nico has a problem with it, he'll tell me." I match her intensity, if not her volume.

"He won't and you know it," she says through her teeth. "He worships you. If you told him to stay until the sun rose in the west, he'd stare at New Jersey every morning."

She's wrong, but she's also right.

"Let's see what happens at Armistice Night."

"You're going?"

"I don't know if she's leverage or if they've washed their

hands of her. Nico can't tell us how they'd react to seeing her... and he can't push them hard enough to force a mistake. Once I know where we stand, we can bring him back."

"It's always going to be something, isn't it?"

"Oria, just stop."

"No. You push people around like pieces on a board while you stay above it all." She's trying to bait me.

"He's staying until I say he's not."

In frustration, she turns her back to me. "I don't know what's with you." She lays her hand on the doorknob. "But you need to get rid of her before you make any more excuses."

I tell myself I will.

CHAPTER 23

SARAH

It's dark when I'm woken by the smell of burned popcorn and thick musk.

"Dario." The squeak in my voice is like a chair scraping. I'm breathing heavily, dizzy from sitting up so fast.

He's cross-legged on the chair against the window, a silhouette against the lights of the city.

"It's rude to stare at a woman in her sleep." The digital clock tells me it's after two in the morning.

He taps his knee. I can't see him properly, but when a draft brushes across my breasts, tightening my nipples, I realize that it's dark but he can see through the thin nightgown just fine.

"I can inspect what's mine."

"You know what I look like." I pull up the covers.

"I know what the *Mona Lisa* looks like. But if I saw it in person, I might stare."

Is he flattering me? My wits sharpen as my head clears. There's no use being angry or offended. He won't give me what I want if I rage for it, but if I turn into a pillar of sugar, he'll get suspicious.

"You should have woken me," I say.

"This is my room. My apartment. My building. And you're mine. I can come in here and admire what I own any time I want."

Admire.

He's already in my bedroom. Maybe now is the time to get this over with.

"You came in here to stare at an acquisition." I let the sheet drop into my lap, exposing the shapes of my hard nipples. "Fine. Then stare."

"Don't get mouthy just because I fucked you." He waits a beat, tapping his knee absently, then stands.

In one step, he's at the end of the bed, and the blue streetlights are reflecting off the edge of his jaw. With one hand on the headboard, he bends over me. I fall back. His breath is sharp with toothpaste, as if he was getting ready for bed before he got dressed all over again to show up here.

"What I came to do"—he runs a fingernail against my jaw, then throat—"is give you a chance to show me what a good wife you are."

He makes a line across my clavicle and down my chest, to the nightgown's neckline.

"You stole a woman, not a wife." My words are breathy and wet.

His face takes up my entire field of vision. His lips hover so close to mine that when they move, I can feel the air around them shift.

"I stole less than I'm owed." He looks down as he traces

past the neckline, over the fabric of the nightgown, and over the bump of my nipple.

The stimulation runs right from my breast to between my legs. It's so powerful I suck in a breath. My eyes flutter closed as he makes a line to the other nipple. His touch is sweet torture. I want him to handle me again. Treat me like a toy he's trying to break. I'll feel bad about losing my way home later.

"Take it again," I say.

He stands straight over me. Maybe to take off his clothes. Maybe to rip the covers off me. The light reveals he's wearing a long-sleeved Henley and jeans. It's a change from the usual. He watches me from that height long enough for me to wonder if he's purposefully presenting a more casual image.

The bulge under his belt is as enormous as it felt when he pressed it against me. Does he think I'm afraid of it? Will he release it or rip off my nightgown?

"I don't want you to hear this in the dark." He flicks on the night table lamp. I shield my eyes from the blinding light. "I'm keeping my end of the deal. I'll allow your brother to see you."

The news is a bolt of energy that gets me up on my knees with my hands clasped between my breasts. I feel lit up like Yankee Stadium. To see Massimo again! To be under his protection, cared about like a treasure instead of a plaything.

Then I realize who I'm talking to.

"What's the catch?"

"I'm not sending you into their arms alone, Schiava. Not so they can grab you."

"They won't." I'm unconvincing even to myself. Massimo would fight for me, and I glow with hope for everything Dario's trying to avoid.

"They'd put you in the *staffa*. You know what that is? Or is your Italian so bad—"

"I know what it is." I was put in the *staffa* before I was promised in marriage. In front of my brother and father, a doctor looked between my legs, put his finger inside me, and confirmed my virginity. It was humiliating.

"Do you know what they'll do when they find out you're ruined?"

"I just want to see them. They won't try to steal me back."

"If they have you, I'll be dead, and they'll sell you off by the piece."

"I don't understand what you're talking about."

"I hope you never do."

"Tell me. I want to know what lies you believe about us."

He looks me up and down, lingering where I'm most vulnerable. "You'll be left in the *staffa* while your men line up to fuck their new whore."

"That's a lie."

Is it? Or is it specific enough to be true?

"They're not what you think. Get some sleep. Armistice Night is in two days. I want you rested."

CHAPTER 24

SARAH

On Armistice Night, Dario sends Dafne with a red dress so bright it's lit from within. I am draped in the color of whores and blood.

The hem flows below my ankles, and the neckline splits the space between my breasts into a fleshy triangle. I won't be able to hide in this thing.

Last year was the first time the Colonia attended Armistice Night. I wore a dress that was just as bright but the optic white of purity and availability. A white meant to broadcast that the Colonia—for the first time in history—was looking to bind itself to another family in marriage.

That night, I was the center of attention. The sun in the sky. Walking in on my father's arm, I was the cause of gasps and murmurs. At first, I hated being exposed. I didn't know the people looking at me, and I was taught to not look back. I could hear them speaking in Italian—a language I had never been taught. My heart was a washer on the spin cycle, turning so hard the rest of me shook and rattled. I wanted to go home. Instead, I went into the bathroom to powder my forehead and reapply my lipstick, remembering what Grandma Marta had told me.

When they look at you and talk about you, it's because you are Colonia. We are the most powerful of all of them. They want you, but they cannot touch you. Don't forget that. We are too powerful to touch.

That night, the men came. I smiled and greeted them politely, but I don't remember any of them. They were too young, too old, and everything in between. Sergio made no impression. He didn't charm me, but that was never the point. He was an Agosti—one of three sons with the correct age and pedigree. They didn't have the most territory or money, but they kept marriage and family in the same esteem and enforced the right way of life with similar jealous secrecy.

Over the next few months, Sergio charmed my father and the men whose opinions mattered. His father, Giovanni Agosti, negotiated territories and succession. I overheard some of it, but the details were crushed under the weight of what was being bartered.

Peter's daughter would be cut into marriage at Precious Blood. A second ceremony under the Roman Catholic Church was allowed but optional as far as Giovanni Agosti was concerned.

What kind of man would exchange his God for power?

What kind of son would he raise?

"Perfect," Dafne says as I stand in front of the mirror. She helped me get ready, unwrapping the dress and putting it over my head so I didn't have to think about it. "Everyone's going to be looking at you."

"Like that's a good thing." My lipstick matches my dress, and when I speak, my mouth looks like an open wound.

"Ready?" Dario says as he walks in, appearing in the mirror behind me before the word is fully out of his mouth. His tuxedo is built for the width of his shoulders and the nip of his waist. His hands look even harder and crueler near the diamond cufflinks that peek past the jacket's sleeves.

Next to him, I don't feel so vulnerable, even though it's his proximity that puts me in the greatest danger.

"I'm ready." I turn toward him.

Dario takes stock of me from my red stilettos with the shiny red soles to the hair twisted and piled on top of my head, then back to my exposed throat.

"Thank you, Dafne." His attention is glued to my body until he notices Dafne is still there. "Thank. You."

"Sarah," she says. "You're better than they are. Don't forget that."

"She won't," Dario growls. "Now go."

She's waiting for me to acknowledge what she said. I do it with a nod.

She nods back and leaves.

"You'll wear this tonight." He takes a box from his jacket and turns me to face the mirror. "Tilt up your chin."

I do it, closing my eyes and holding my head high as he lays something cold against my throat. After a click, he lets his hands skate over my arms as they drop. I look in the mirror. I'm wearing a wide platinum-and-diamond collar with a lock in the center. It curves at the top, under my chin, comfortably preventing me from looking down.

Dario touches the collar at the back. "There's a ring

here." He yanks it a little so I know he's telling the truth. "I'll have a leash with me. Don't make me use it."

"What can I do? It's Armistice Night. All feuds are put to rest."

"We'll see." He runs his nose along the edge of my jaw. "Don't underestimate what a man will do for a woman like you."

"Because I'm stolen property."

"What man wouldn't want to have you?" His finger draws along my neck and shoulder, leaving a crackling line in its wake. "You're beautiful. Graceful. Loyal. Honest. I stole you for revenge, but you're a prize worth taking."

Pushing the neck of the dress away, he exposes my breast and brushes against the hard peak.

My blood has changed since he made me into a woman. I was stiff and brittle, and now I am viscous, moldable, yielding, warmed by the soft spark of his touch.

"Rule four," I say thickly. "I'm not loyal."

"I know." His lips kiss across my back while his hand caresses my breast.

"You can't make me loyal by fucking me."

"Maybe not." Fully behind me now, his erection presses on my ass. "But I can make you come."

He doesn't make another move. In the mirror, he watches from over my shoulder, waiting for something.

Me. He's waiting for me. When I swallow, the muscles in my neck press on the high collar.

"Make me."

He does not hesitate.

"Bend at the waist, Schiava." He gently pushes me

forward. I can't look down, so I have to trust him. "Put your hands flat on the mirror."

I'm fully bent, but my neck remains straight. Now I can only look down at my ankles, where the red dress is lifted away.

"I'm going to fuck you from behind." Slowly, the skirt is lifted over my waist, exposing the red lace garter that came with the dress. "My cock's going to go deeper." He pushes down on my lower back, then lifts my hips until I'm curved for him. "If it hurts, you will tell me immediately. Understand?"

"Yes."

He unsnaps my underwear, and his huge palms cup my ass, pulling me open from cheek to thigh.

"These should be apart." With the tip of his shoe, he taps the insides of my feet. I move them so I am spread, bent, curved, and collared. He takes his hands off my bottom. "You're still abraded."

Unable to look up, all I can see is his shoes behind mine while the clink and whip of his belt and fly tell me he's taking out his cock. His feet step closer, readjust, and I feel the rigid smoothness of him invading my folds.

"And wet," he says, rubbing himself against my clit.

"Yes," I moan as he stimulates where I'm most sensitive.

"I didn't ask anything."

I push back toward him. "Yes anyway."

His chuckle is barely audible, but there's real appreciation in it rather than cruelty or sarcasm. "You're a good woman." He slowly enters me, stretching the muscles in a new way. "Too good. They're all going to want you. They'll try to take you to get in your father's good graces." Slowly, he draws himself in and out until, with one hard thrust, he's hit the wall.

I squeak in pain. I'm supposed to tell him when it hurts, but I want him to hit the end again.

"Keep going," I gasp. "Please." I want to feel this. Feel everything. I can't pretend getting here didn't hurt.

He's as likely to punish me for telling him what to do as he is to take requests.

Instead, he reaches around with one arm and flicks my clitoris. When I let out a long moan, he continues, fucking me deep, only hurting me when I push back against him.

"I want you sore tonight," he says to the rhythm of his moves. "Fucked and sore."

Keeping his hand on my clit, he takes the ring on the back of the collar and pulls me back. The shock takes my breath away, and in that moment of thoughtless distress, a crack opens, and my sense of my body's place in the world gets sucked through it.

He lets go of the ring, and I drop. Standing takes more will than I have. Balance is too complex. His arms, his cock, and the space around me—thickened with pleasure—hold me up.

"You're so close, *principessa*." He lightens the touch between my legs. "You want to come before I mark inside you."

All I can release is a *nnh*. I want to come, and I would, but he's modulating my pleasure with expert fingers. And also... but...

"Rule five," I say through gritted teeth. "It doesn't matter what I want."

"So perfect," he rumbles. "Come for me."

Using his fingertips, he flicks back and forth against my nub, every stroke a little detonation, then a bigger one, until they overlap in a white-hot explosion that stiffens my knees and sends the contents of my lungs out my mouth in a cry against, into, and from this drowning oblivion.

When he takes his hand away, he also pulls out. Empty and noodle-limbed, I collapse into his arms. He lays my back on the mattress, his frightening, shiny cock bobbing as he takes off his pants. Crawling onto the bed, he opens my legs wide before entering me again.

I'm sore already, but I take him deep. When I touch his face, my fingertips lingering on the flat tops of his ears, he pulls my hands away and pins them over my head.

"Tonight, when they see you," he says, "they won't know my body has been deep in yours. And when I drip down your leg, you'll know I own you."

"I already know."

"Know again. And again." He drives into me, then turns his face away.

By the pulse and rigidity of his body, I feel him empty into me, then he drops, letting my hands go.

Letting my hands drop, I don't touch his ears again. Not even when he kisses my cheek and gets up on his hands. My legs drop, but he pushes them up and open again, reaching under me to grab my underwear so he can yank it off.

"I have to go to the bathroom to clean up." I reach for the handful of lace.

"Did you not hear me?" He slaps my ass and reaches between my legs to gather two fingers of wetness. "You're going with me dripping down your fucking leg." He drops my legs and wipes the thick pearl on my lips. "And my taste on your mouth." He gets up. "Don't lick it. Don't wipe it away, or I'll tan your pretty ass in front of everyone."

He gets his pants on, straightens himself, and stuffs the underwear in his pocket.

When I stand, my dress falls over the raw, despoiled, tender parts he's claimed. I can smell our mingled juices on my lips. Everyone else will too.

CHAPTER 25

SARAH

D<small>ARIO DRIVES</small>. I <small>AM IN THE PASSENGER SEAT</small>, <small>THINKING ABOUT</small> telling Massimo I want to come back. Would he take me home with him? I'm no longer able to marry Sergio and bind two territories. Maybe I'd be humiliated and treated like a pariah for being ruined by an outsider, but I'd be home.

And there's no staffa. No line of men. That's an absurd fairy tale for a sick mind.

"What's going on in your head, Schiava?" he asks casually at a red light. "You look like you want to jump through the windshield."

I do. My insides are coiled to leave my skin behind.

"I'm excited to be out."

"The rules are the same."

Rule one. No questions.

I'm already an expert at getting around that.

"You wouldn't be taking me out unless I'd earned your trust by following the rules, so I find it strange you think you need to remind me," I say.

"Rule four remains to be obeyed."

"I haven't done anything to make you suspect I'm disloyal."

"You've lacked opportunity. That changes tonight."

The idea of change and opportunity makes my heart flutter. "And you're allowing it. You must trust me."

"Or I'm testing you."

"What if I fail?"

"I won't be far. If there's a moment you can't see me, that's when I'll be closest."

"You're making me nervous."

"I haven't had to worry about a man looking at you. You're going to be in a room full of traffickers and dealers. Any one of the men would violate you at the drop of a hat, and the women wouldn't give a shit. So, good. You should be nervous."

Dario pulls onto Chelsea Piers and shows his ID to the guard. We appear to be the last to arrive. They have a short conversation in Italian, but all I can do is stare at Dario.

The arm lifts, and he drives slowly into the lot.

This year, Armistice Night is on a yacht owned by the Messina family. It's docked at Chelsea Piers, with layers and layers of security. At a black carpet, limos line up and valets open doors. There's no music. No shouts from photographers. Just the sounds of the lapping water and evening city to accompany the orange wash of sunset. Just the raw burn between my legs and the wet sting and tickle of another drop slipping down my thigh.

"Why are you still looking at me with your mouth open like a tin can?"

"I don't know why you're bringing me to this." I sit

straight. "You could have brought me shopping or to the park or something first. But no. You hold up your end of the deal and let me see my family, but somewhere I can't really talk or enjoy being outside or anything."

"Hold on." He stops by the valet and holds his hand out so they don't open the doors right away. "You wanted to get *outside*?"

My scarring hand sits in my lap. The wedding ring has twisted around to look like I'm holding a snowflake in my palm.

"I want to see them. But being here..." I take a deep breath. "Now? I was irritated a minute ago, but I realize... now... that I'm not in that suite or the greenhouse anymore..." I wave my hand at the windshield, toward the world at large. "This. Yes. I want to be in this under any circumstances. I don't have a vote in anything, but I'll face a room full of bad men just to get out of that prison."

"Okay."

"Okay, what?"

"If everything goes well tonight and you're good, we can go to..." He stops, like a warden who has no idea what a prisoner would do with freedom.

"The park?"

"Sure. Or shopping. Or out to dinner."

I laugh to myself.

"What?" he asks.

"Nothing." I'm looking down at my hands again. My thumb pushes the diamond snowflake to the front.

Dario says nothing for what seems like a long time. When I look up at him, his expression is as open as a set of double doors at the end of the hall.

"You've never been to a restaurant." His words are spoken without the intent to hurt, but they're salt on the rawness of my inexperience.

"It's not a big deal."

He squeezes my knee and pulls it to him. "Open your legs."

Three words melt me into a puddle of submission. My knees relax and spread apart.

The valets wait on either side of the car.

Dario slides his hand up my skirt and unceremoniously runs it along the length of my seam.

Yes, I'm sore.

Yes, his actions are rude and degrading.

And yes, my back arches at his touch.

He removes his hand and sniffs the fingertips. "You said you want me to teach you how to be a woman."

"I do."

"Only another woman can do that." He spreads the slick gloss over my lips. "But I can teach you how to go out to a restaurant."

Before I can register disappointment, he kisses me. I'm stunned. Frozen. Eyes wide open, vision blurring into a foggy windshield, until his tongue seeks mine. My lids shut against the flood of desire and warmth. Together, we taste the juices from between my legs against the softness of our lips and the rough twisting of tongues.

He pulls away, smiles at me, and raps his window twice.

The driver's side door opens. Dario gets out, leaving me open-mouthed and taking half breaths, and crosses in front of the car on the way to open my door for me.

He moves like a king who owns the entire world and is beautiful inside it.

Did that kiss mean anything more than the sex?

Were we sealing a deal? Communicating anything at all?

I hate him.

I want him.

Dario helps me out of the car. Finally, under the cloudy sky, I breathe deeply. The air smells like ozone, salt water, and car exhaust. He leads me over the black carpet and helps me over the uneven gangway. We're checked and verified by men in tuxedos. When we step onto the boat, the gangway's lifted, and we give up land for the Hudson River.

We're led down a hallway and into a small room with a couple dozen people in it.

"Careful." Dario points at the raised lip of floor.

I enter the lush space where everyone's shedding their coats and handing them off to the service staff. I am alone in this crowd. They all know what happened to me.

I untie the waist loop of my coat, and Dario peels it off my shoulders. That's when everyone seems to stop talking. Mouths close. Eyes open. Are they looking at my dress? Or the collar with the lock? Are they waiting for my husband to leash me like a dog? Maybe they see or smell the spunk wiped over my lips.

"Chin up," he whispers from behind me. "Remember, you're mine."

Dario takes my hand and kisses it before leading me through the crowd. Unable to look down, I have to make eye contact with strangers. Only the most important men from the most important families will attend tonight, along with their wives. I seek out Massimo and my father. Will

Grandma come? What about the Agostis? Will I see Sergio? Can I gauge all their reactions right here, in the coat check room?

The lock at my neck clicks against the collar. None of the other wives are wearing streetwalker red or a collar with a lock and a ring for a leash.

Head up, though. Head up.

I let Dario guide me. He pauses at the doorway, murmuring, "Step up."

The floor is two inches higher. I would have tripped.

"Thank you."

Last year, Armistice Night was held at the ballroom in the New Amsterdam Brotherhood of Police HQ, which had a utilitarian simplicity about it, so I'm not ready for the lush carpet or polished bronze. Windows overlooking the river and moving skyline bracket a ballroom under two massive crystal chandeliers. On the other side of the room, toward the front of the ship, two bartenders work behind a teak counter that's lit with soft, warm lamps.

As the crowd enters behind us, servers with silver trays pass out drinks and pinch-sized bites of food. Half a boiled egg with stripes of red over the swirled yoke lands under my nose.

"Aioli egg with red peppers?" the waitress states and asks at the same time.

Last year was a buffet. In my kitchen the next day, I told Denise every luxurious and glorious detail. This is ten levels above that, and I'm not sure what to do.

"Yes." I'm trying to hold her here, but I can't see a fork or a plate, so I look around to see how everyone else is picking up their food. Napkin, fingers, napkin. "I got this." I say my thoughts out loud, then imitate the other guests. Napkin, fingers, napkin.

"You don't need me to teach you anything." Dario refuses the food, sending the waitress away with a glance. "But you're still mine. Don't forget it."

"How could I?" I eat the egg in one bite, overfilling my mouth. I cover my lips until I can swallow.

"Is this..." A voice rises from behind Dario. He turns, revealing Sergio, with his casual charm, dirty-blond hair swept to one side, clean-shaven and bright-eyed, in a tuxedo that's tight around his football-player build. "The newlyweds!"

A walnut forms in my throat, too big to swallow and too hard to crack.

"Congratulations, Mr. Lucari. On the wedding." Somehow, Dario and Sergio are shaking hands like gentlemen. "It's been a while, but I see you've won her over." He makes a face, indicating my collar as if being forced to wear it could be proof I've been charmed. "I never took you for a ladies' man but..."

"He's no ladies' man." My father appears beside Sergio in three stilted steps. "He's a fucking pickpocket."

I want to run to my father and beg him to bring me home. My body has other ideas and leans into Dario as if my body can see what my heart is still blind to.

Daddy seems different. Not older, though there's a bit of that, or thinner, though his jowls are a little less full. His eyes look smaller, shiftier. The ring on his pinkie seems more gauche, and his voice is filled not with love, but violence.

He hasn't changed. I have.

"I'm not here for the flattery," my husband says.

"Right." Sergio smiles again as if he finds Dario truly delightful. "Okay, so like I was saying, impressive. I mean, the whole effort." He holds his hands out to contain the entirety of Dario's plan and its execution. "Jacking the Town Car. Picking her up on our wedding day. Convincing William the Doorman you were legit. I mean, wow. To hear him tell it, you practically... I don't know, tied him down and kidney-punched him until he bled piss. Which..." He shrugs. "That sounds weird, am I right? We tested the bleeding piss idea and... Well, there's a reason the big dummy spent forty years opening doors for a living. He mixed it up. You don't bleed piss. You piss blood." He turns to my father. "What was it he said? 'I'm dying,' something-something?"

When I met Sergio, he was funny but not jokey. Smart but not overly erudite. None of that fits with the blood-and-piss story. I'm supposed to believe they really beat William that badly—and I do.

"Something about pain," my father replies, confirming they hurt a man who looked after me for over ten years just because he didn't verify that the right driver was in the right limousine. Daddy's looking at Dario as if he can't wait to make him piss blood, then at me. "You all right, baby girl?"

I haven't been "baby girl" in a long time, so I don't answer right away. The dynamic of the conversation has changed because the question is so bland on its face and hostile in tone. I can't tell if he actually cares.

"I'm fine, Daddy."

"How much," Sergio says to Dario softly while he thinks I'm distracted by Daddy, "for a video with a view of something besides the back of her head?"

Dario's expression darkens. He looks like a man who's never smiled a day in his life, and it's terrifying. He's got a gun, but everyone here does. This is not a place to get into a fight over me or anything.

Is that what's behind me being here? A massacre to discredit the Colonia just as we come out of the shadows?

"Don't do it," I whisper.

Dario doesn't insult me by asking what I mean.

"How about a drink?" My husband offers me his arm, and I take it obediently, letting him guide me to the bar. "You all right?"

"I'm fine." I can't help scan the room for Massimo. I don't see him.

"You look like you ran out of here and left your skin behind." With gentle pressure under my chin, he turns my attention to him.

"Really. I'm okay."

"What do you want to drink?"

"I, uh..." I swallow against his hand and the collar. I've only ever had one kind of alcohol. "Wine. White, please."

"Have another egg." He takes his hand off my chin and calls over a waiter with a flick of his wrist. "Take two bites this time."

The waiter brings his tray. Napkin. Egg. Egg. I can't fit a third. I'm biting into the first egg when a man's voice greets my husband.

"Lucari."

Dario shakes hands with a man I've never seen before. He's handsome, unshaven, wearing an open collar under his black jacket as if he shredded the memo about the event being formal.

"DiLustro," Dario says. "What's with the tan? You look like a half-Greek starfucker."

"I was on my honeymoon." He puts a hand on the back of a short woman with curly black hair and eyes as dark as his. Her floor-length dress is sparkling black and has a neckline that plunges between her breasts.

"Did you take her to the *best* Italian backwater?" Dario asks.

"California," the woman talks around a mouthful of egg, then swallows. "Don't change the subject. You have shit to answer for."

I'm shocked and a little terrified, but Dario is unfazed by the accusation, deciding to introduce me instead. They are Santino and Violetta, and he tells them I am...

"Sarah. My wife, Sarah."

It's the first time I've heard him say my real name. Not Schiava or *principessa*. It is music on his lips, and my pleasure at hearing it is greater than the sum of its syllables.

Sarah.

"I..." Can't speak. Lost in his eyes. Between my name and the way he's looking at me as if I'm the only other person in the world, I'm both confused and unafraid.

"Sarah Colonia?" Santino asks.

"Yes." I snap out of it. Paste on a smile. Meet the gaze of the man asking the question. "My last name was Colonia."

"I heard." He sips his whiskey. "I just didn't believe."

"What did you hear?" I ask, looking from him to his wife, Violetta. She's staring at the collar, then meets my gaze.

"I have to go to the bathroom." She grabs my wrist. "Girl rule. You have to come with me."

CHAPTER 26

SARAH

BEFORE I HAVE A MOMENT TO OBJECT OR ASK DARIO IF IT'S ALL right or apologize, Violetta pulls me through the loose crowd, down a short hall, and opens the oval bathroom door.

"Wait!" The ship rocks, and I'm thrown forward, tripping over the lip at the entrance. A grab for the towel rack keeps me from falling.

Violetta slams the door. The single-user bathroom has a marble sink and frosted-glass sconces in the shape of Corinthian columns, but it's very small.

"Whoo, boy, I gotta go." She gathers the skirt of her gown around her waist.

Turning, I face the mirror and open my clutch. A tube of lipstick, a compact, nothing more. I take out the lipstick. In the tiny room, the sound of Violetta peeing is as loud as a fire hose.

"So," she says. "I saw Dario at the end of August. He didn't say he was engaged."

I twist the tube. Say nothing.

"Not that Santino told me he was engaged when I met him. To me. Engaged to me. I found out on my wedding day." She rips off toilet paper. The hose is turned off. "So, I guess I shouldn't have expected Dario to mention it, but..." There's a rustling beside me while I redden my lips. "There's kind of this rule in the Cavallo family now. Like, recently."

I press my painted lips together, intending to tell her that the rules aren't really my business, but suddenly, she stands next to me in the mirror, dress properly placed, and finishes her thought in a dead serious tone.

"A new rule about running this kinda thing by me."

"I supposed to do something?"

"Not you." She washes her hands. "Dario."

"He was supposed to ask Santino?"

"Me. Ask *me* if he could... Look, maybe the rule only counts in my territory, but Dario was in that territory not too long ago, and he has three of my guys, so if this is what I think it is..." She slaps off the faucet and pinches a towel off the pile. "This shit is not gonna fly."

"I don't understand."

"Did you fall in love, accept his proposal, and consent to walk around in a collar, then get married? No judgment if you did. But if you didn't?" She throws the towel in the basket. "You're coming home with me if we have to shoot our way out of here."

I don't know how it's possible, or why it's even a story she's telling herself as she fixes her hair in the mirror.

"Santino doesn't even know me."

"Sweetheart. I'm in charge." She clicks through items in

her bag, pushing past a gun to get to a tube of lipstick. "If I say go, we go. Just say the word."

My mouth is agape, but no words come out. My brain is as clean as Violetta's hands.

This is what I wanted. Prayed for. She can save me. Do what my family refuses to do.

"Sarah." She uncaps her lipstick. "Say the word."

This woman will take me out of here and protect me. Take me where she lives, where I'll...

I'll...

What?

Does it matter?

Yes.

How far away?

No.

The word.

Say the word.

Please.

The door bangs hard enough to send us both back, gasping. But it's not a bang. Just a knock. Violetta zips her bag closed and slides open the door.

My father stands there with his arms crossed, tilted a little to the left. "I thought you was dead in there."

Violetta holds up one finger. "The men's room?" She turns the finger horizontal. "That way. The one with the little pants man on the door."

No one has ever spoken to my father with this level of venomous condescension.

"Then you should use it." He lifts a finger and points at me. "She's got a meeting with her brother."

Daddy reaches past her and pulls me out. I trip over the

little lip again, and in the moment before I catch my footing, when I feel as though there's nothing under me, I shout to Violetta.

"The word! The word!"

I'm screaming, but I'm still being dragged down the hall.

THE ROOM IS BORDERED by windows dotted with diamonds of light. They flash a blue so bright it turns night into dusk. There's a bang in the sky. Rain. Lightning. Thunder.

I'm alone on a beige semicircle couch facing a fireplace where a line of flame rises from a bed of broken glass.

Fifteen minutes watching the flames. Did Violetta hear me? Was she messing with me? Was it all a joke?

Or did I just get Dario killed?

Someone comes in. I don't move. I'm afraid to.

"Sarah."

In front of the flickering firelight stands a man. His features are obscured, but I know him. I've known him my whole life. I rush to him, arms out for an embrace, but he holds out his hand. I freeze in place, mid-run, like a statue of a woman trying to catch a bus.

"Massimo?" I ask, relaxing my arms and putting both feet on the carpet, raising my chin because the collar forces me to.

His gasp is barely audible over the hum of the boat's engine. The sound of my name in his voice cuts me to the bone. For a moment, I forget why I'm here.

"What has he done?" Massimo steps into the light.

"Please, Emo, take me home."

181

His eyes glint in the firelight as he scans me back and forth, full lips clamped tightly enough to hold back a hundred angry words. "Home? To what?"

He's not stupid. He's being intentionally thick, and I can't tell why.

"You'll have some power after tonight, right?" My breath hitches as I try not to sob.

"Sarah." His voice is gentle. I know then that it's a lost cause, but I can't stop.

"After the succession ceremony, you can take me back. I talked to a woman. Violetta, she says—"

"No, no, no. She's weird, okay? Don't talk to her."

He's utterly dismissive of my only sliver of hope.

"I miss you. Denise and Grandma and even Daddy. Their voices in the kitchen and the way we all knew what we were supposed to do."

My palms are sweating, but when he takes my hand, he pretends not to notice. "This is what it is, Goody. We got lazy, and we lost. I learned that. We're going to scrub the streets with him, but you?" He shakes his head. "You can't come back."

"There has to be something I can do."

"It's that bad? Come on."

Stunned, I pull my hand away. "How can you even ask that?"

"You can't make the best of it?"

"You're a monster. No better than him."

His mouth twists into a tight line, and his finger juts out at me.

"You were always this way," he roars. "Always your way. Always pushing. You made Grandma fucking crazy."

"You did whatever you wanted while she beat me constantly."

I've never said those words. Never called the corrections beatings. Never complained or implied I didn't earn every stroke.

I'm more shocked by my words than Massimo, who replies without taking a breath to absorb what I just said.

"You never learned how not to get beat!"

He's right. I learned how to do what I was told, but I never learned how to navigate the trap doors that got me into trouble. Never learned how to see around corners or anticipate the moods of those who had authority over me. I've done it all wrong my whole life.

I drop to my knees, extend my arms in front of me, one hand flat on the carpet, the other grasping the red clutch. My forehead rubs against the rough wool. I can sink lower. I can drop right through this floor and into the sea if that's what it takes.

"Goody! Get up!" Massimo hisses in a whisper that's also a shout.

"Take me home!"

He does what I hope he'll do and kneels beside me. "I can't—"

"Get up." It's Dario from behind me.

I don't have a chance to decide if I'll obey before he's pulling on the ring on the back of the collar and yanking me up. My legs akimbo, one stiletto sideways, I can't quite get my feet under me.

"Don't pull her like that," Massimo growls.

"I'll pull her"—he yanks me up until I'm on my feet—"any way I want."

"He's right," another voice comes from above me. It's Daddy. "Come on, Massimo. We got the ceremony."

"Yes, Peter," Dario says. "Let them know who gets the power when I murder you."

My father casually waves his thick hand. "You, somebody else, fucking lightning outta the sky. It don't matter. That's what you ain't getting. Something's taking me out, and I ain't facing one direction looking for it. I don't give a shit who kills me. That's why I'm on the ground, not under it." He addresses me. "Be good, peanut." Daddy starts out of the room but stops when he realizes my brother won't leave. "She's one of his now."

One of his?

One?

"Just like her mother." Daddy's last words are muttered like an afterthought and dropped like a bomb.

Suddenly, I've lost contact with gravity.

CHAPTER 27

DARIO

SARAH'S FATHER AND BROTHER ARE GONE.

We are alone in that room.

She should have been under the table at my feet. I should have put her on a leash and made her heel all night.

It didn't have to go this way. Oria said as much. But instead of playing it safe, I played a game of risk. Now I have won a dangerous prize in a flaming-red dress.

Sarah Colonia has gone volatile. Uncontained. Her control has slipped away. I see the division before that second Sarah—the one stifled and chained her whole life— even speaks a word.

It's over. In that split second, my power over her has reached its end. I overplayed my hand by a few words out of her father's mouth.

I don't care. I've never cared.

But here I am, watching the docility slip off her as she turns to me, eyes piercing my skin and slicing me open,

185

cauterizing the wound so the rush of blood doesn't obscure the contents of my soul.

I care. Fuck. Fuck this. Fuck the Colonia. Fuck it all.

I care.

"Sit down," I command because she looks as though she's ready to launch in all directions.

I can't explain what's going on when she's standing there, looking through me. She remains still yet everywhere. Deadly kinetic.

Why am I afraid?

"Sit down!" I growl.

Standing in that red dress and platinum choker like an imprisoned warrior, she disobeys. Again.

If she wants to know what her father meant, she's going to have to obey. Sit the fuck down. Then... how can I tell her? I consider lying. Saying her father is making things up and I don't know what he's talking about. But I shouldn't have to lie. I have nothing to apologize for.

I will take her by the hair. I will drag her to her knees. I will tell her what I want to tell her and no more. She will demand nothing, and I will take everything.

But she does not sit. The boat rocks in the rainstorm. I set my feet wide. She stumbles in her heels and grabs onto the back of a chair.

"Do it," I add, indicating a spot on the couch. "I'll explain."

Muffled sounds come from the dining room, through the walls, unintelligible as anything but the announcement that Massimo will succeed his father as head of the Colonia now that the oldest daughter is married.

"You. Will. Explain." Her tone is intolerable. I step toward her, and she holds up a hand. "Don't touch me."

Has her voice always been that feminine? Before she spoke with this flat affect, I never noticed. The combination is powerful. I have to shake it off like a drug that could turn into an addiction.

"You asked him to take you home. You'll be punished for that."

"You will explain."

She can't ask questions, so she's phrasing them as demands. Rule one backfiring in my face. It's all collapsing, folding around me like an envelope, and once I'm sealed inside, I'm done.

"You will sit."

When she moves, I'm sure it's to obey, and a flood of relief gets dumped into my system.

But she doesn't sit. She walks past the couch and to the side door that leads to the deck. Without pausing, she slaps down the lever and slides the heavy door aside, rushing out as if I'm going to chase her out there and drag her back by the ring on the back of her collar.

And I will. I'm faster, and my shoes are flatter. But when I grab for her, I wind up with a fistful of cold air. The deck's a few inches lower, and when her feet don't find the floor where she expects it, she falls as the boat rocks, taking three long steps into the railing, bent over to face the dark sea.

Adrenaline floods where the relief was, and I grab her arm to keep her from falling over.

"Get inside!" I shout over the wind, then deliver the weather report like a fucking idiot. "It's pouring rain!"

"No!" She wrenches away. Her shoes slip on the wet

wood. Grabbing the top of the rail, she pulls off her right shoe. "I am not"—she flings it into the water and reaches for the left—"one of many."

"You're not." I go toward her, but she wields a red-soled heel at me.

"My mother! Deny it. Deny it so I can call you a liar."

"I didn't kill her."

"Liar."

The light from the windows shifts. A shadow crosses her face. There are men in the room with the curved couch. After-dinner drinks with a side of Dario and his stolen, rain-drowned wife. I'll have to bring her back in though another door.

"If you'd just come inside, I'll explain it."

"I saw Willa's postcard." She jabs her shoe in my direction. "What are you? Some kind of *pimp*?"

"No." I'll explain in the goddamned rain if I have to, but she doesn't let me.

"My *mother*." Her wet dress sticks to her so tightly I can see the lace pattern of her bra. "Do you think I want an explanation? Some excuse? You raped her and didn't mean to kill her? Is that it?"

My God, is that what she thinks?

"Come inside." I touch the hand she's rested on the rail, and she pulls it away.

"If you ever touch me again, I will kill you." The boat rocks, but she regrasps the rail. She doesn't need to. She won't fall. Her anger levitates her. "I don't know how or when, but you'll be sorry. I'll poison you. Stab you in your sleep. I'll rip you apart with my teeth."

I back up. She's not going to kill me, but having me near

is only making her angrier, and I don't know what she'll do next. But I watch. I won't let her out of my sight.

A man comes out with an umbrella. I expect Massimo, confirm to myself that she's not going home with him. I will not negotiate for my wife, nor will I give up on the destruction of the Colonia.

But the umbrella moves, and light hits the man's face. It's not Massimo.

It's Sergio.

CHAPTER 28

DARIO

THE DECK IS NARROW ENOUGH FOR SERGIO'S UMBRELLA TO COVER my soaked, shivering, enraged wife in one step. It's been a split second since she threatened to rip me apart with her teeth. I'm still frozen in place, wondering how to handle this ferocious animal I thought I'd tamed, while he touches her bare shoulder.

Maybe it's his pinkie ring with the big A in diamonds or the way the rain drips down her arm. Maybe it's the way his umbrella protects her while I let her soak up rain. Maybe it's that he's already started talking and she's *listening*.

I'm probably on edge from this whole event going to shit, or maybe I just don't want this fucker touching my wife while he says things I can't hear.

My hands itch so badly that pulling out my gun and shooting him doesn't even cross my mind. The umbrella easily slides from his grip and goes flying into the wind. He's looking at me, and I realize I might just kill him. My head stays

190

clear when my fist hits his face with a wet slap. He hits me back, but I don't feel it. Not really. Sarah's crouching by the plexiglass rail, and it's the danger to her that keeps my head about me. When he hits me a second time, I step back to clear Sarah and to let Sergio think he's getting the upper hand.

Stepping away from her, smiling, he tries to punch me a third time.

"Short fucking arms." I duck out of his reach.

Then I let the rage blindness overtake me and fall on him like a ton of bricks. Soon I'm holding him over the rail by the throat, bent over the storm-stirred river. His face is red and wet, eyes bulging.

"She's mine." I choke him.

"Stole..." He barely gets the word out.

"Dario!" Her voice cuts through my rage, but the wound heals as quickly as it's made.

We're surrounded by black suits and umbrellas. As long as I don't take out my gun, I'm honoring the armistice. I'm allowed to kill this fuck with my bare hands. Knowing this is like riding downhill on a newly paved street. The wind is the only friction.

With a swipe of my foot behind his knees, I could send him overboard, but he doesn't belong to the river. He belongs to *me*.

I throw him to the deck, and he tries to get up.

Fuck that.

I go for him. Sergio lunges for my legs, but I saw that coming a mile away and kick him in the face, which he handles the first time, but he's not prepared for the second kick, which sends him flying on his back. My pants get cold and wet at the knees as I straddle him, fists to face, punching past his grabbing hands.

"You think you got something." I grunt as I hit him. "Soft little bitch. Don't know what to do without a gun." He's not struggling anymore. I can't stop punching him. "Think you can take from me. I was born into shit. Fought my way out."

"Stop it!" Her shout navigates around my rage, and though it's the first one I hear, I know she's been screaming it over and over since I pulled Sergio off the rail. "Stop it!"

Obedience isn't my job. It's hers.

"Stop it!"

But she cracks my shell, and the anger leaks out.

I stop, leaning back, letting my bloody fists fall to the side. We're coming into port. The lights of the city are softened and haloed by the cloud over the city. This entire clusterfuck is over. My arms ache. My jaw throbs from clenching. My chest and gut—where he got a few good shots—hurt when I breathe. The rain washes Sergio's face clean. His nose is crooked, and his left eye is swelling shut.

You should see the other guy.

Whatever demon possessed me is gone. I won't kill Sergio tonight.

Silence has replaced the cries of *stop it stop it stop it.*

Where is she? I spin to a standing position, feet apart, ready to murder anyone who's silenced my Schiava. My *principessa.* My Sarah.

But she's where I left her, dress soaked, hair wet, lips quivering in rage, and shivering with cold, a tuxedo jacket over her shoulders. Keeping her warm and protected is my job, but her brother is the one with his umbrella over her.

Since he's in his shirt, I can only assume that's his jacket over her shoulders

She thinks she already hates me. When I tell her the things I've kept from her, she may hate me forever.

I wasn't supposed to care how she felt about me, but I do.

Approaching her, I take off my jacket.

"Thank you," I say to Massimo as I slide his jacket off my wife's shoulders. He takes it. "Don't fuck with my marriage."

She looks at me with her jaw tightened against chattering teeth and eyes that challenge me to confirm all her worst fears.

Her shivering is unbearable. I drape my jacket over her. She seems to draw it around her shoulders for a moment, then lets it drop off. I grab it before it lands. The dress sticks to her curves, her hard, pointed nipples, the crevices between her legs.

I punch my arms through the sleeves, checking for faces that judge and eyes that lust. The foghorn blasts. We're docking. There's no time to fight.

Quickly, I bend and pick Sarah up under the knees and shoulders, carrying her out.

"I told you not to touch me." But she puts her arms around my neck and melts into me in exhaustion and tears.

At the coat check, people are looking. Word of where I bloodied my knuckles is getting out. No time for coats.

Sergio's already by the ramp with his arms draped around two men, and I'm blocked by fucking Violetta DiLustro.

"Get the fuck out of my way." I say it quietly, because

I've already pushed my luck with Sergio's face. Another scene on this boat will deadly.

Santino's right next to the woman who runs his fucking life. "My wife wants to speak to yours." He lights a cigarette with that big, clacking Zippo.

"Sarah." Violetta draws too close. "You said the word."

"I just want to go home," Sarah mutters. "Please let me go home."

"We can take you."

"Home." She holds me tighter. "Let him take me."

Violetta steps back and holds her hands up to Sarah, then addresses me. "This isn't over."

"You're in my territory." I hold my woman close. "It's over when I say it is."

As soon as my feet touch land, Sarah wiggles away and drops into a lopsided run. One shoe was lost.

Cursing under my breath, I follow her, patting my pockets for my wallet and valet ticket.

Shit.

She took them when she had my jacket.

Pushing past everyone, I catch sight of her running across the parking lot, toward my car, which was last in, so it's the first out.

Barely stopping, she shoves something into a valet's hand. He nods and tries to ask her something, but she's a red streak in the floodlights, opening the driver's side door. The fob will be on the dash, but does she even know how to drive?

The headlights go on, and I get in front of the car.

It moves with a jerk and fast—right at me.

She doesn't know how to drive. I don't move. She's going to stop, or she's going to hit me. I almost wish she'd run me down.

The tires slide a little when she jams the brake, stopping so close to my legs I can slap the hood. Our eyes meet past the rain-dotted windshield. She's in control of a weapon she doesn't know how to use, and she's scared.

"Put it in park." I jab a finger toward the gearshift at the center console.

She looks at it, then back at me, then back down. She shifts. The car unlocks, and she slides into the passenger seat.

I can manage this. I can manage her.

I get behind the wheel without looking at her or the small crowd of criminals and their wives in evening wear.

"Get this thing off me!" She grabs at the collar.

I unlatch it and throw it in the back, then drive out of the lot. Sarah curls up on the passenger side, looking out her window and saying nothing while I blast the heat.

"You want to know about your mother," I say.

She doesn't answer right away.

"When my mother died, my grandmother told me she'd help for a while and she'd teach me. But I was the woman of the house now. I'd have to do everything she'd done. Cook, clean, take care of Massimo. Grandma didn't say it, but being the only person to love me was my job too."

At a light, I put my hand on her back. The skin is still clammy and cold. She shrugs me off, and like a pussy, I put both hands on the wheel.

"I was seven, and I learned everything Grandma taught me. But I never learned how to love myself the way my mother did." She looks at me. The light on her cheek goes from red to green. I pull into the intersection. "Did you take her away from me?"

"No."

She's crying, sniffling with breaths sticky and wet. I reach inside my jacket for a hankie and hold it out. She does not take it.

"Are you the outsider who raped and killed her?"

"No!" I'm not ready for the parking lot yet. I pull the car over half a block from my building and lean into her body, which is turned away as far as it will go. "Sarah, listen to me. No."

"Don't lie, Dario."

The rain is a curtain over the windows, closing us into a muffled cocoon where it's safe to tell her dangerous things.

"She's alive."

She bolts up straight and turns off the heat.

"That is a lie."

"Your mother ran away."

"Liar. She'd never leave me!"

"She had to."

"My father and my brother just turned their backs on me. I'm cast out. I'm nothing to them. I have no one. All I have is the memory of the only person who loved me, and you're defiling it."

"I found her. I helped her."

"That's Oria's story." She holds up an accusatory finger. "You're stealing it and using it to lie to me."

"It is Oria's story, and it's your mother's, and—"

"Where is she?"

"I don't know."

She stares at me, and I'm not sure who I'm dealing with until she opens the door and gets out.

"Shit!" I follow her, water flowing over my dress shoes. "Wife!"

I call to her years of learning to do nothing but obey. She continues east with one bare foot, head bobbing with her uneven gait as she hustles into the lobby of my building.

Of all the places she can go, she runs right back to where I kept her.

At first, this pleases me. I'm fooled into thinking she wants to be where I am, and knowing I am fooled does not dilute that moment of pleasure.

I catch her inside the elevator.

"What did he mean, 'one of his'?" She's shivering again.

"You're mine. That's all you need to know. I'm not explaining myself to you."

"You're a monster!"

The doors open and she rushes out. Connor catches her.

"Take her to the suite," I bark.

"No!" she snarls. "The greenhouse."

"The suite. It's going to be freezing up there."

Still, she repeats the demand with more vocal force. "Take me to the green*house*." She ends at the top of her lungs, spitting, eyes bulging, lips curled over canines.

"Fine." I'm calm. Too calm. "Take her to the greenhouse."

Sarah's body goes still, and the look of satisfaction on her face says that despite my best efforts, I've met her worst expectations.

CHAPTER 29

SARAH

AT FIRST, I AM ANGRY.

Not just angry but consumed by rage so hot I kick off my one shoe and walk barefooted around the perimeter of the freezing tile floor. Frost grows in the corners of the glass rectangles, and the moonlight reveals the clouds of my every exhalation.

Dario Lucari is going to pay for his lies.

The only light from inside is the red eye of the camera. I ignore it.

I let my skin goose-bump, then go bluish white. The soles of my feet tempt the newly swept floor. My nipples harden to rocks.

With every step around the perimeter of the greenhouse, I plot my course. I'll bite his dick off. Slit his throat with a sharpened fingernail. Twist his balls and make him scream. He'll murder me, but I'll join my mother in death...

Except...

No. Except nothing. He's lying.

Except...

Daddy had confirmed what I hadn't been told yet. My mother might not be dead. She could be anyone. Anywhere. Walking the earth or buried beneath it.

Unless Dario's lying about not knowing where she is.

Fat raindrops plop on the glass and drip a few inches.

If my mother's alive, she's not Colonia anymore. She's severed.

Are You My Mother?

Am I the little bird, or is my mother?

Which one of us wanders the earth looking for her place?

"It's all a lie," I voice unintentionally. The words are a habit of denial, but I know they're hollow. I face the camera. "Why are you *lying*?"

Everyone on the other side of that lens knows what I won't accept.

The truth.

Where is my mother?

When I put my palms on the glass, the sweat on them goes cold. The falling sleet rattles against it in surrender. It's the rain's job to fall, to splash, to melt, to drip, to die. By morning, it will all be the mist that shrouds everything past Sixth Avenue.

Are You My Mother?

Is she out there somewhere?

Does she want to see me?

Am I free to find her now that I'm as good as severed too?

I'm a prisoner, but I'm free.

I press my hands on the glass hard enough to feel the sheets of cold rain.

It's not vertigo that keeps me from moving, but another kind of spinning. I've been looking through a paper towel roll my whole life, thinking what I saw in the little circle was all there was, and now, with the possibility of my mother alive in the world, the cardboard is shredded and I can see what's around me. The feeling of disorientation is almost physical. I can't move. If I stay still, it's about my mother. If I take my hands off the glass, I'll be overwhelmed by the possibilities.

The only obstacle is Dario. He won't trust me. Not yet. But what if he does? Will our marriage always be a prison?

What if he lets me go? What would that mean?

I can do things.

I can go places.

I can want whatever I want.

I try to clutch at something before I fall, but the glass is cold and flat, and I slide to the floor, crushed under the burden of freedom.

CHAPTER 30

DARIO

AT THE CLOSED-CIRCUIT MONITORS, WATCHING SARAH PACE THE greenhouse, I promise myself she will never get that close to leaving me again.

I'm not sending her away.

Not letting her see her family.

She's mine.

She turns into shimmering pixels drained of warmth, getting still as she drops to the floor. She'll sleep it off. Back away. We'll take care of it. Nothing to see here, kid. Just dots and dots and dots...

"Sir?" Oliver's voice cuts through my fugue. His big eyes are narrowed with concern, but he's looking at the same screen I am. All I see are frozen pixels.

I widen my view. She wrestles with the wet dress, peeling it away. Then her bra goes. It's fucking cold.

Guilt turns my blood to ice water.

I push past Oliver and run to her, smacking open the door to the stairwell, taking the steps two at a time. My breath explodes into clouds as soon as I burst into the greenhouse. It's dark and as cold as I expect.

Sarah's hunched on the floor, naked, blue in the moonlight, muttering a nonsense song through lips that release the faintest clouds.

I gather her in my arms. "I have you."

From some territory on the wrong side of consciousness, she replies in words that no language will claim.

I rush down the stairs. Now that I have light, I can see her blue lips, the shiny alabaster of her skin, the dead weight of her head as it bounces in my arms. I hold it steady as I back into the lock bar across the door to the penthouse hall and into the suite, where I should have forced her to go in the first place.

"You're going to be all right." I lay her on her bed and cover her with every blanket I can find. "I swear. Nothing's going to happen to you."

Against the back of my hand, her nose and cheeks are cold. I won't dare unwrap the blankets to check the rest of her. I call her by her name for the second time, and I'm ashamed it had to come to this.

"Sarah, please." I'm panicked but not surprised when she doesn't answer. "God damnit." I jerk up to standing. "This is taking too long!" I slap open the closet door. I don't know what I'm looking for, but I swipe out everything. Stacks of towels. A summer blanket. "Just give me a minute. I'll fix it."

I am a monster.

When I come back out of the closet, she's unwrapped herself, murmuring things I can't understand. She strong, and cold, and resistant.

"Sarah? Oliver said you—" a woman's voice echoes from the hall. "What are you doing?!" It's Dafne.

"Blankets!" I shout.

Without hesitation, she pulls a wicker basket out of the closet. It's stacked with blankets. Obviously. Why would I know where the blankets go? That's a woman's business.

"Where?" Sarah grips my arm, wide-eyed, then drops into lifelessness.

"Good," Dafne says with relief. "That's good."

"What's good about this?"

"She won't throw these off." She tosses me a blanket. We layer them one after the other, until it seems the weight will crush her.

"What now?" I am not in charge. I am a child in over his head with adult matters.

"I'll heat up some broth."

Dafne goes to the kitchen. I should go to the control suite and see if there's any word from the Colonia or the DiLustros. I don't need this many enemies when she's sick. I need to make calls. Send someone somewhere to do something.

There's no way in hell I'm leaving her.

I do something I haven't done my entire life—I pray.

But there's a reason I've never asked God for any favors. He doesn't deliver, and prayer is boring when I have everything I need to answer my own damn prayers.

I curl up behind my wife to warm her body with mine. I feel the snowflake ring on her finger. The metal is cold. It slides off easily.

Her teeth chatter. I bend to see her face. Her lips quiver, then the color returns to them.

Or the other way around, because though my body is where it should be, my thoughts are thrust backward in time. Under a wood chipper, with a naked, freezing woman between my brother and me. I'm an ignorant boy again, convinced I'm not giving her my warmth but stealing hers for myself.

"No," I mutter through gritted teeth. "That's not how it works."

But it is. I am incapable of giving or healing. I can only take and wreck.

"Sarah."

She shivers in response, her body trying to replace the heat I'm robbing.

"I'm sorry."

As I pull away from her, she sucks in a breath, and as I stand, I hear something that could be an exhale, or it could be a word. I lean in so close to her face I could kiss it if I dared. Her lips are moving, and when a word comes out, I jump back.

"Yes!" She agrees with such shocking lucidity I assume she's awake, but her eyes are still closed. "The bunny's in training, and it's not a mother. It's Father Falcone."

As if that makes perfect sense. I get out of the bed.

"What is he going to do to my fingers with that knife?" she continues with a childlike animation that only serves to accentuate the emotional flatness of her voice.

"Dafne!" I call with all the authority I've earned. "Get in here!"

"You are not a father," Sarah says as Dafne rushes in. "You are not a teacher. You are not boss of me."

"It's the hypothermia," Dafne says. "Keep her warm and—"

Sarah throws off the blankets and sits up, eyes still completely closed. "You are not a cock or a cunt or a sneeze."

"What's happening?"

"Cover her!" Dafne gets the blankets up, and I grab my wife and lay her down.

"You are a *snort*." Sarah struggles against us. Her skin is still cold to the touch, but warm enough for her nerves to work. She fights to get my hands off her.

"It's okay," I say. "Just—"

She thrashes, elbowing her teacher in the face and straightening her leg suddenly, which lands her heel in my balls. I grunt and curl. Sarah jumps up and stands naked on the bedroom rug, her hair a nest and her eyes bloodshot, just as Connor walks in.

"Crikey."

"What?!"

He's looking at her naked body without a speck of desire, and lucky for him, because I'm in the mood to throat-punch a guy.

"Just checking in, so..." He jerks his thumb in the general direction of anyplace that's not here.

"You are a snort!" Sarah screams at me. "You are a snort!"

"Get out!" I roar at Connor, who doesn't need to be told twice.

"Where am I?" Sarah cries from someplace in her head. "I want to go home!"

"She's delirious." Dafne reads the doubts in my mind.

"Normal with hypothermia. She needs to be under the covers."

"Okay." I turn to my wife. "Sarah, listen—"

"You are not a cow or a car or a pig or a *staffa* or a chicken..."

Sarah goes on and on, sometimes limp, sometimes struggling, but Dafne and I wrestle her down. After a moment, as if she's forgotten why she was fighting in the first place, she lets us wrap her up again.

"You are a snort," my wife sobs. "And you are my mother."

———

I'VE PULLED one of two matching chairs close to the bed and perched myself on the edge in case I need to leap off it to protect Sarah from the demons in her mind.

The only way I'll leave her side is if they burn down this entire fucking building. I don't care about the Colonia right now. Revenge doesn't need me to rescue it or watch its sleep turn restful.

The thermometer beeps.

"Ninety-six point three," Dafne says. "When she wakes up, she won't remember anything."

"I should send her home like she asked."

Dafne *tsks* and shakes her head.

"Delirium's normal for hypothermia." She puts her hand on Sarah's head. "So's stripping down... Increased blood flow to the extremities creates a hot flash. Some people, in the final stages, they dig and burrow."

"I'm sorry?" What she's said activates a file in my mind, but I can't open it.

"They take their clothes off and dig a hole or hide under something."

"Like what?" The file's opened, but I can't bring the information into focus.

"Some just hide under the bed. It's really quite bizarre." She stands. "We're lucky our charge here didn't get that far."

"Yes." I bend, leaning my elbows on my knees, and run my fingers through my hair.

"You seem to be having doubts." She sits behind me in the matching chair.

"I'm not a monster."

"No. You're not." Fabric rustles. Dafne could have a gun to my head, but I can't take my eyes off Sarah. "You don't trade girls into sexual slavery. You don't tell them it's legal or threaten their families if they don't comply. You don't break their minds before you—"

"Enough," I whisper, and she falls silent.

"What you're doing," she finally says. "It needs to be done. You're the only one who can stop them. They won't make the same mistakes twice. No outsider's going to get this close ever again. You have her." The chair's springs squeak. She's leaning forward. "You can't give up."

Leaving my elbows bent on my thighs, I look at her. "Dafne."

"Sir." She sits back, remembering her place in my pecking order.

"She didn't beg to be rescued the way you did."

"And I'm grateful." She crosses her legs and plants her hands in her lap. "She will be too."

"You can't free someone by force."

"I disagree."

Turning away from her, I unbend, sliding down the chair. I can see her silhouette in the dresser mirror.

"You're not even free of it. You begged me to get you out, and there's still a part of you that wants to go back. You're *still* one of them in your blood. It's going to take you the rest of your life to shake them. How long is it going to take her? After the way I did it? She's never going to be free. Ever."

"She will." Dafne smooths her palms over her thighs and stands. "And when she's ready, you're going to free her so all of us can be free."

It's too dark to see the details of her face, but we make eye contact in the mirror.

"You're dismissed," I say.

She leaves without argument.

The night passes in silence as I struggle to connect the dots of my present with the lines of my past.

CHAPTER 31

SARAH

MY HUSBAND STROKES MY HAIR, KNEELING BY THE SIDE OF THE BED.

Who is this man with the tender voice, and why does he look like the animal who stole me and starved me?

I squeeze my eyes shut to clear them because something isn't right. When they open, it's still Dario.

"What happened?" I break rule number one.

"You were soaking wet. It was a chilly night. And I left you there to punish you. I knew better, but I did it anyway."

I don't ask him why because I'm not allowed to ask questions. But more than that, this man who looks like my husband already has regret written all over his face.

"You became hypothermic." He shakes his head and sits on a chair that's set close to the edge of the bed.

"Then what?"

I'll ask questions until he stops allowing it.

"I brought you down here."

"How did I get naked?"

"I've made a lot of mistakes with you."

"You mean bringing me to Armistice Night dressed like a whore in a collar?"

He smiles ruefully, leaning forward with his elbows on spread knees. "That's the least of it."

"I thought you did that so my family would reject me."

"I did." He clenches and unclenches his fist, cracking the crusted blood on his knuckles.

"Well, it worked."

"Not the way I wanted." He straightens up. "I'm going to tell you everything."

"Everything?"

"Everything I can." He stands. "There's a lot, and some things are secrets for a reason. But I won't lie."

"And I have to believe you." I sit up and squint at him, but I can't get this man into focus.

"I'm not forcing you to do anything anymore."

He says it as if it doesn't matter. I can believe him or not. My choice—and one I didn't ask for. At least when he was torturing me, I knew where I stood even if I didn't know anything else.

But the bread is baked. Its life as dough, as flour, as wheat and seed, is long gone. Once the nourishment's taken, hunger will return.

"When does it stop?" I get out of the bed and stand before him.

His thumb and knuckle play with the bottom of my fourth finger. I look at it. My wedding ring is gone. It must have slipped off.

"I'll make it stop. Soon."

"You're going to ask me to believe things today and how

many tomorrow? What happens when I believe you so much I forget who I am?"

"I'll remind you." He locks our eyes and hands.

"No." I pull away. He's in focus now. My husband and purpose, pulling me into an unknown life I wasn't raised to live. He says I have a choice, but I don't. "It's too much, too soon. Please. Give me a minute."

He obeys as if I could ever set out the rules.

IT'S NOT until I finish my shower that I realize I woke up believing Dario.

It sinks in as I get dressed in the things from Dafne's pink bags.

I believe my mother ran away, or was cast out, because I remember her clearly.

She was trouble. She raised her voice when she defended my drawings to Daddy. She read books to us that sent Grandma into a rage. She embroidered me a steam shovel. She cried when she wasn't supposed to, and she refused to cover up her tears for my father or anyone else.

She said no one ever left the Colonia, but Dafne is here, and I was thrown away.

My father's half-truths are only half his sins.

I assumed I'd been told everything worth knowing. Willful ignorance has been my sin.

You'll always have us, Sarah.

We are yours, and you are ours.

My wedding ring is gone and only the scars remain.

I don't belong anywhere anymore.

My face splits open, shattering into a spray of gasps and spit, tears coming so hard they fly away from my cheeks. I can't breathe. I can't move. I can't stop.

Being taken away from home was hard. Understanding that I might never go back was harder. None of that compared to having the Colonia taken from my heart.

I cannot unsee, unthink, unhear what I know now. I can't pretend the community I grew up in never existed.

My whole life has been a lie.

Where do I belong?

Who have I been?

Who am I now?

Do I even exist?

Did I ever?

I crawl out of the shower into the bathroom, on my hands and knees, submitting to no one, crying at my own funeral.

Grandma said to wait until the crying was done and the tear ducts ached.

Then put a cold compress on your eyes so your father doesn't find out I had to do this to you.

She made me cry, then taught me how to cover the evidence of my weakness.

Don't distress our men. Don't spread your misery around like a disease.

In the Hell's Kitchen bathroom owned by the outsider who kidnapped me, I cry on the floor as though it's my job. The tile is cool on my cheek and soon wet with tears from ducts that are going to swell and hurt. It pours out until I'm hollow inside.

I'm as much human as a geode is solid rock. One good

whack and we crack open to reveal that the shell is the only thing of substance or value.

I don't hear the suite's front door open. I don't hear Dario's footsteps. I don't hear anything until he calls for me.

"Sarah?" His call from the living room cuts through the clogging in my ears.

I try to respond with an apology for failing again, but my throat is hoarse and phlegmy.

Then, before I can do anything, he rushes into the bathroom and crouches by me, hand on my back. "What happened?"

His voice is startlingly affectionate, but when I try to catch a glimpse of that tenderness on his face, his mask is back in place again, distant and unreadable.

He grabs my wrists, looks inside them, checks me all over, stretching me on the bathroom floor as if I'm a car he's thinking of buying. Under my arms. My ankles. My throat. He puts his ear to my chest to confirm it's empty.

Dario is on one knee. The other is bent with his foot flat on the floor. He leans forward with one hand on the tile by the fingertips and the other on my forehead as if he's ready to either caress me or spring into action. He's a ceiling over me, protecting me and preventing me from standing. I don't want to get up. I want to lie here and die here.

Grandma promised me men hated women crying, but he doesn't seem angered by my weakness. Another lie. Or maybe my husband just doesn't care if I'm crying. I prefer that.

"I have nothing." I tap my chest as the tears start again. "Empty."

"Oh, Sarah." He rubs his thumb along my cheek, stretching a tear. "We all are."

We are?

He kisses me where the tears have fallen, and there are so many for his tender lips, his cool nose, his hard, rough chin. His tongue finds mine, and my hands discover he's hard where I'm soft, built up where I'm split apart, giving where I am constructed to receive. Kissing and kissing and kissing, our bodies slide into place, me under him, my head pushed against the tile, my legs around his waist for him to push the shape of his erection against my soft insistence. Moving against me, his tongue thoughtlessly shifting, he grabs what he owns, taking the hard nipple between two fingers so tightly it hurts.

"I can't stop myself." He groans into my mouth, then sucks in a breath. It's hesitation. I won't allow it. I can't stand it.

I reach down for him, rubbing the club under his clothes, trying to find a way in past the wall of clothing he's built around it, while he unlocks me with his fingers. I am shut up like a cave after a rockslide. No light. No air. A stone-coated vacuum, and his hand sliding past my waistband down to where I'm wet is everything in the world, groping and grasping, finding something hard enough to break me against. Finally.

"Let go."

His words are more than permission. They are purpose.

My orgasm is a heaven of empty, hard-shelled pleasure lined with jewels.

"You all right?" he asks when my eyes open and I'm panting under him.

"Thank you." I put my hand on his cheek as a prelude to an apology that—with a kiss—he tells me I don't need to make.

His watch beeps.

"Who's NL?" I ask.

He shuts off the beeping.

"Get dressed," he says, helping me up. "I'll explain in half an hour."

CHAPTER 32

DARIO

I CLOSE THE CONFERENCE ROOM BLINDS AND SLIDE OPEN THE PANEL that covers the small screen. Check my watch. Oria enters, right on time.

"How is she?" She sits next to me and takes out a compact to pat the shine off her nose.

"Fine." I address the physical but say nothing about what just happened on the bathroom floor. "It was a rough night for her."

She nods and catches sight of my hands. The knuckles are starting to scab.

"Jesus Christ, Dario." She goes back to the mirror. "You left it all on his face."

"He had it coming."

"For what?" Oria snaps the compact closed and slides it into her back pocket.

The small screen flickers on, relieving me of the burden of explanation.

"Good morning!" Nico's hair has been trimmed to a

216

manageable mop. He's in a tiny room with no windows. Behind him, a dot matrix printer pecks and clicks.

"I like the hair," Oria says approvingly.

"Thank you. I like the face."

These two have been together for years, and they still make me ill.

"How is it over there?" I ask to keep from throwing up.

"Teepee and a wigwam," he replies with an old joke from childhood. "Two tents" sounds the same as "too tense." He addresses me. "What the fuck did the Agosti kid do to you?"

"He exists." They just look at me, waiting for the real reason. "He touched my wife."

"How exactly?" Nico asks, always precise. "Hand up the skirt? Finger brush on the tits while making a point?"

He was checking to see if she was all right. Not sexual at all, but that isn't the point. The touching was what set me off, but the thing that undergirded my reaction was the umbrella he was providing and I wasn't.

"Enough that I had to shut it down," I say. "If I let him get away with it, he'd feel entitled to shave my territory. A block here. A block there."

"Before you know it, he'd be fucking your wife?" Nico says.

"I did what I had to do."

"You pissed them off. They were looking for you, sure, but now they're on points over here, and the Agostis are making an alliance even without the marriage."

"They won't find us," I say.

"They will eventually," Oria adds.

217

She's right, but "eventually" isn't something you can count down on calendar.

"We have time," I say.

"Really?"

"She's going to give up information she doesn't even know she has. The boats. The routes. We'll be in place to choke the entire trafficking side of the operation."

"You're stalling." Oria points at me as if she can shoot fire through her fingers.

"He's right though," Nico adds.

"Of course you take his side." She pounds her fist on the table. "Whatever big brother says."

"Boo, honey." Nico tries to calm her with pet names. It doesn't work.

"If she has information, then use the goddamn phone!" Oria snaps at me. "As long as she's here, he has to stay there to protect her. Fuck that. Put her on a plane. Get her out and get him home."

"She's my wife, Oria."

"Oh. My. Fucking... She is not. That wedding was as legal as spitting in your palms and shaking hands. How long are you going to play footsie with her? Treat her like an adult. Tell her the stakes and write out a questionnaire. Her mindless obedience is the point of the entire thing. All you're gonna do is fuck with her head while, back at Cult Central" —she points at the screen, meaning the Colonia—"Nico, your brother, a.k.a. the love of my life, is a sitting duck for people who'd kill him if they knew him. The job is done, okay? It's done. We fucked them, and we'll continue to fuck them until every girl they're abusing is out. This is a long game. Don't play it short because your dick twitched."

She sits back, done but not done. If I let her, she'll go on until Nico gets an agreement in edgewise. Once they're aligned against me, I'll have to do twice as much arguing over where Sarah's going.

She's not going anywhere.

Period.

"We'll send her away when it's time." The effort it takes to not bark is more telling than the barking would have been. "Not a minute sooner."

Oria flops back in her chair, beaten.

"Nico." I keep a tight lid on my wildly swinging emotions. "Is there anything immediate you need me to pry out of her?"

"Ask her where they keep the Ho Hos. I cannot eat another sausage."

"I hate you both right now." Oria presses two fingers to her temple. It's all body language. Nico's miles away, but she knows how to get to him.

"Okay, I have to say something, as your brother." Nico pauses, waiting for me to switch gears.

"Fine."

"You're not in love with her."

"I know that, but how do you?"

"She's useless. She's qualified to be a wife—that's it—and not a competent one. Ask her if she knows how to balance a checkbook. Drive a car. Make a doctor's appointment."

"Maybe that gets me off."

"You've only ever loved one woman," Nico says. "And she was *competent*. She ran circles around you."

"I'm not in love with anyone. This meeting is over."

"She's not going to make it," Oria adds. "When we destroy them—she's destroyed."

"Thank you for the reminder." I look at my watch as I rise. "There're eleven minutes left in the call. You two spend it however you want."

I leave them to it before I have to defend myself further.

SECURITY IS ARRANGED. The Audi is prepped. My heart is steeled against the habit of secrecy.

I'm about to tell Sarah things I never had to promise myself I wouldn't. Why would I when I have nothing to gain from revealing where I come from? She has no need to know what motivates me or why she was targeted. Even if I trust her, even if she never goes back to them to reveal details of my life, I still have nothing to gain from revealing it all and everything to lose.

She stands by the elevator in a long, black skirt and a thick cable sweater. Her single braid is neat over her shoulder, and her lips are pink enough to fuck.

But I won't. Not now. Not even to stall and distract. She needs to know who I am, and she needs to know why she's here.

"Hi," she says nervously. "No one was out here, so I figured I'd wait."

"It's fine."

"Where are Vito and Gennaro?"

"They belonged to Santino and Violetta. They've gone back."

"Like I belong to you?"

"Not like that." I touch her cheek for no reason but every necessity. "I needed men who wouldn't be recognized."

The doors slide open, and we get in.

"Press L," I say.

She does it without hesitation. "What's P?"

"Parking. And all the numbers in between are the floors, if you want to stop there."

She hits a bunch of random buttons. The car stops.

"That's not okay." I push DOOR CLOSE.

She responds by hitting 7, 6, and 5, lighting the panel like a Christmas tree before I grab her hands and pin her wrists to the wall above her head.

"What?" she asks with a coy grin. Her cheeks call to me, pulling my lips to brush against their warmth.

"You're slowing us down." I kiss her face and jaw, letting the elevator stop on the next floor and move on. "This kind of behavior," I say between kisses, "is a social perversion that will not be tolerated."

"But it's fun." She doesn't pull her arms out of my grasp until I let her go. Then I use my keycard to reset the buttons.

"Benefit of owning the building."

"Is it bad, really?" The car picks up speed. "Like, rude? People don't like it?"

"Generally, no."

"It's just..." She looks away, seemingly bewildered by something she's feeling. "I never got to press the buttons or do anything. I don't even know how they work, really. Not until now, which is... I guess..." She runs the ovals of her mittens over the buttons without pressing hard enough to make them light up. "I was never out of our apartment or Precious Blood alone. I was escorted or driven around, which is no excuse. You shouldn't have to tell me something so simple, but thank you."

"Sarah." I take her hands in mine. "You don't have to be ashamed."

"I'm not. I'm..." She thinks a moment before the elevator stops at L. "You're right. I'm a little embarrassed."

"Now you know, so you don't have to be anymore."

"Good." She nods. "Good. I'm glad it's not that hard."

In the lobby, she touches everything. Shiny metal railings and rough stone planters. When I open the lobby door, the wind blows loose hair away from her face, and she blinks hard against the wind before walking through. Her brown eyes are translucent in the sun.

"I know this corner." She points at Moishe's across the street. "The deli there. I know the swirl on the M." She gazes at the sign as if she's seen it but never looked closely enough to appreciate it.

The parking lot gate clatters, and the Audi comes up. Connor gets out.

"I'll be right behind with the Jeep," he says.

"Good." I walk around to the passenger side but don't make it halfway there.

Sarah's gone.

A fist of fear clenches my gut, squeezing away my ability to think, or breathe, or see anything except a life without her.

She's neither left nor right. Neither east nor west. There are too many people. Too much movement.

I'm losing her.

It's pointless. The traffic moves through the intersection. She's gone.

Lost. Forever.

Across the street.

Right under the Moishe's Jewelry sign, staring up at the swirling M with her bronze braid hanging down her back, and I'm a fucking idiot, jogging across 47th, trying not to laugh at myself.

"Don't do that," I say. "Don't just walk away."

"I've seen it a hundred times," she says about the M, ignoring me. "But not like this. Only through a car window, and it was tinted, so I had no idea the red was so bright. There are so many people out. They're walking different places in different directions. And the cars, they're everywhere. I've seen it all before, but being right here? In it?" She tears her gaze away from that invisible point to look at me. "It's like there aren't any rules, but it's like the elevator, isn't it? There are a ton of rules I don't know, and they're not that hard."

"There are." I put my hand on her shoulder to ground her, but she ends up grounding me. "I'll teach you."

That's never been my job, and I know it, but while her nose and cheeks are autumn pink and one loose hair blows across her lips, she's mine. No matter what Oria thinks about where Sarah should go next or when, no one else can do this job.

"I feel stupid." She puts her hands in her pockets.

"You'll learn fast." I pull a strand of hair from the corner of her mouth. "And I feel sorry for anyone who tries to stop you."

Her attention drifts to the red M in Moishe's, and she shakes her head absently, not refusing me but something she's suggested to herself.

"I don't belong anywhere."

My car coasts along the West Side, and I'm going to tell her things I haven't even told myself.

"You belong with me." I take a second to change my mind, then use the time to find the courage to stay a course paved with risk. "No matter where you go, I will come for you. I'll find you, and I'll take you back. Once you know how to live in this world without me, you'll know you belong with me."

I'm promising more than I've ever promised—or been able to deliver—to any woman, but she's the only woman I've ever needed to promise anything.

"I don't know how to get where you think I'm going in life."

"If you stay close, I'll take you anywhere you want to go."

"Okay," she whispers.

For a moment, I don't have a single doubt in my mind or reservation in my heart. She is mine to guide, and she'll be fine.

CHAPTER 33

SARAH

How big is the city?

Manhattan is almost twenty-three square miles, but I don't know the vertical square footage. No one's counted the whispers a hundred stories high or the shouts buried with the long dead. They don't count the secret places built over a few hundred years.

It's easy to stay in the confinement of experience and ignore the locked doors in public places, the tunnels and alleys, the stacks of floors and ceilings, but out with Dario, my curiosity about the things I can't reach turns into fascination.

"What are you looking at?" he asks, driving the black Audi that I failed to drive off the Chelsea Piers parking lot.

"The city." I notice how the top floors of the oldest buildings on Sixth have more ornate trimmings and smaller windows, as if the architect needed to punctuate where the structure met the sky. "It looks different."

I envy his ease in his body and in the world. He knows where he belongs while I feel alien to myself.

"It's not." He drives quickly, navigating the lanes with a nimble austerity. "You're different."

I'm so focused on Dario, considering the power of his body, the way he wields it, that even after he turns us south and east and the neighborhood turns to tall brick buildings arranged around a grassy park like prehistoric sentinels, I don't recognize the neighborhood.

Only when a black squirrel darts up a tree, incongruous in color yet exactly where it belongs, do I realize we're in Stuyvesant Town.

We left here when I was ten, and yet I am home.

My muscles turn to stone, and my lungs stop working as if exhalation will bring the next moment, when I find out this was all a test and I failed. Or I'm being bartered back. Or my chance to learn how to live never existed.

"Dario," I squeak airlessly. I grip the armrest. I don't want to go back. I know too much, and I don't know enough. I'm still in between.

"Hey." He sees me as he turns his head to park on the street. "You're white as a sheet."

"You're bringing me home," I babble as he backs into a tight spot on the 14th Street service road.

"What?" He puts the car in park, looks at me, forehead knotted, then outside, and his expression relaxes. "No. Sarah, no. You're not going back."

"Are you sure?"

He levels his eyes to mine as if to reassure me of his sincerity.

"Yes. Cross my heart. I want to bring you someplace."

"And you're not leaving me?"

"I grew up here too. I want to show you something."

He kisses me. The door locks clack open.

Over his shoulder, Connor's across the street. I look out the front. Two men down the block are trying to look casual getting out of a car.

Dario gets out, leaving me alone for a moment, which is how long I have to catch my breath. He crosses the front of the car, looking everywhere, scanning the world for pending trouble. He opens my door and helps me out, then lets my hand go.

I follow Dario to a blue kiosk with a P on the side.

"Gotta pay the man." He slips a card into the slot. The numbers on the top change.

"Can I do it?"

"Press the green button. Two hours should be enough."

"A restaurant?" I push the green button until there's a number two on the left. "That's two hours or two minutes?"

"Hours." He offers me his arm. I take it. "When we're done here, we'll get something to eat."

He guides me across the sidewalk and into Stuyvesant Town, another world of spindly, leafless winter trees and tenants in long coats, bundled against the chill.

"At a restaurant?"

"Slow down." He puts his arm over my shoulders, guiding me around a blond brick building. "You asked me why. Why you? Why the Colonia?"

"I did."

"I'm going to tell you." He turns another corner until we're behind the building, where the custodians keep a staging area for cleanup equipment. "We used to call this Junktown."

"They still never finish with the Christmas trees before the following Thanksgiving." I point at the drying pine and fir trees stacked against the wall, some with sprigs of silver tinsel still webbed between dry needles.

"No. They don't." He walks over to the wood chipper where the trees will mulch their fates. He crouches, looking at the bottom. "This one's newer. They used to have a space under them."

"I remember," I say, recalling it all in a flash. "There was a litter of kittens under there once, but Daddy said it wasn't safe to get them."

"It's not." He looks at his shoes, then up at me. "My mother died there."

The information is so unexpected I almost forget my manners and cry, *What?!* But real compassion rescues me from discourtesy.

"I'm so sorry, Dario." I want to hold him, this man who kidnapped me, ripped me away from my life, stripped me naked, and made me beg for a sip of water, but he doesn't want comfort. He exudes the energy of a car speeding by so quickly you remember it as staying still.

"We were a sublet. The guy who had the lease—my mother called him Old World. Kind of secretive. We were evicted. Three of us. Mom. Me. My brother, Nico. The rent was paid, but..." He shrugs.

"I don't know much," I say with unearned confidence, "but I don't think you can be kicked out like that."

"New York City, Division of Housing and Urban Renewal Rent Stabilization Regulations. Chapter Eight. Subchapter B

—Part 2525 sets out rules for subletting which are limited to two years, except under Part 2523.5, which excludes family members as defined in section 2520.6(o) who are entitled to be named as a tenant on the renewal lease." He crosses his arms and nods sharply. "Lot of old Colonia used to live in these buildings."

I know this because I grew up here, with Grandma pulling me away from outsider children in the playground.

"My..."

Father?

Me.

And I finally understand what all of this is all about.

It was me.

But I have to say it out loud. To make it real.

"This is the building where I grew up."

"Yes, it is. My mother sublet it from your grandfather's estate until your father was ready to move in with his family. Which turned out to be in January. No warning, no help, nowhere to go. We huddled behind the Christmas trees. Nico and I went looking for food, and when we came back..."

He turns his gaze up; the day's light is fading fast, and the windows are lit to a cozy yellow glow.

I wonder who lives here now. Who's putting dinner on the table, unaware of the horrors that have occurred in this little yard.

"She was naked, under a wood chipper. We tried to keep her warm. We thought she was raped and left for dead, but you..." He shakes his head and puts his hands in his pockets. "You taught me that's not what happened."

"How?"

"When you were hypothermic, you stripped down."

"I thought you did that." I laugh.

He touches the bitten-off tip of his ear, an unconscious gesture. Even if he didn't wear its scars, it's clear from the tension in his body, the ache in his voice, that the eviction still lives in him. It's driven everything he's done since.

"Come on." Dario pushes a code into a keypad by the service door and snaps it open.

For a moment, I just stand there looking at him, imagining the boy he was, shivering and terrified, his entire world collapsing around him. That hunger to survive etched its desperate lines into his face even as the rest of him grew tall and strong with shoulders square and set. His coat and shoes are expensive, and he carries himself like a man who knows his own authority and power. Whoever he was in this dump of a yard has been erased by the man he is today. The man he's made himself into.

Dario leads me inside and closes the door. The dark room smells of acrid solutions and thick, stinging concentrates. I trip on a mop bucket, sending wooden handles clattering to the floor.

"Sorry."

"It's all right." He's a shadow picking up brooms and mops and leaning them against the wall, between two open wall boxes vomiting wires.

He pulls me out the next door into a thirteen-story stairway shaft without a ceiling and slides open the service elevator. We get in, and when he pulls the lever, we shoot upward like a rocket. I'm grateful for the coat; it's not a particularly cold day now, but I wouldn't want to be out here without it. And as the wind bites my cheeks, I wince with sympathy, imagining being cast out in the unkindest weather with nowhere to go.

"Your ears," I say when the toothy wind hits my own ears.

"Frostbite." He's looking toward the top of the open shaft, afternoon sun on his face, hair blowing. "Tips of my fingers too. They found Nico and I trying to keep our mother's body warm. We didn't find out she was dead until after they amputated." He rushes to the next thing so fast sympathy dies on my lips. He doesn't want it. "Brace yourself. This thing stops like a—"

The car comes to a screeching halt at the top before he finishes. He lets me out first. As soon as I step onto the roof, the sensation of those days when I lived here comes rushing back to me: how free I was with mom.

"This was my favorite part of the building," Dario says, walking to the far eastern edge, looking out past the taillights choking the FDR to the dark expanse of the East River, and Brooklyn on the other side. "In the summers, when it was too hot to breathe, my brother and I would sleep up here, under the stars. The mosquitoes were terrible, but that made it more like real camping."

"I loved it up here too," I confess. "Sometimes I brought a pad and pencil, and I drew whatever I wanted, then I took every page and threw it over the side." I make the motion of throwing a balled-up piece of paper off the roof. "Even the good ones."

"That's a real commitment to littering."

"I didn't want to get caught with them." I glance at him to see if he's reacting to my past defiance.

"You won't throw away any more drawings," he says. "And you won't hide them."

Instead of agreeing or thanking him, I look away, unable to digest this change in life. "After my mother died, I was the woman of the house. But up here... I could imagine doing anything."

"What did you imagine?"

I haven't allowed myself to think about any of this in so, so long. "I'd daydream about the boats and where they could take me. Hopping on the 6 a.m. ferry and going on an adventure to Greenpoint. It felt like the other side of the world. Or stowing away on a cargo ship and ending up somewhere brand new."

"That 6 a.m. ferry." He laughs without any cruelty lurking at the edges. "It woke me every morning."

Without quite meaning to, I've drawn closer to him. The two of us are standing side by side with our forearms leaning on the cast-iron railing, hands hanging into space, our shoulders almost brushing. We aren't looking at each other. Somehow, that makes it easier to confess.

"All my happiest memories are here," I say. "All of us lived here together. This is where I had a family. We moved to an apartment with space for Grandma after Mom died. But this—it still feels like my home."

"Mine too."

"NL? The alarm on your watch? That's Nico? Your brother?"

"Yes."

"Where is he now?"

He tilts his head, looks over the view, considers his

answer, then replies, "I could tell you, but I'd have to kill you."

"You wouldn't."

His thumb lingers along my bottom lip before he takes his hand away. "Nico and I were in the foster care system. Sometimes together. Sometimes not. But always... we knew someone was going to pay for what they did."

"My father," I say. The answer to all of it was in those two words.

"More than that. The family—the system—that sent my mother to die under a wood chipper."

"So, you found us."

"First, we found each other." He shakes off some lingering hesitation. "We were separated in foster care. Then we found out what we needed to know. We were ambitious. We were relentless. We learned all about you people."

"Us people?"

"With your secrecy and your twisted rituals. You're a bunch of inbred deviants, and I hated you. I still hate you. All of you." He looks at me. "Not you as much. You I'll keep."

Does this mean he's not sending me away? I can't ask.

"Thanks. I'm honored."

Dario's mouth is set in a thin, firm line when he says, "You've been brave, Sarah."

"That's so interesting because I thought I was weak." I count descriptors on my fingers. "A slave, a whore, and a useless princess." The last one counts for two.

"You forgot beautiful, and strong, and clever. You were raised to hide yourself. They drowned you every day, but you're made of fire."

His grudging approval means more to me, I realize, than my father's most lavish praise.

There's a long moment of quiet between us. Up here, the city feels as if it's far below us, a sparkling mass of light and noise we can observe from on high.

This conversation with the monster who kidnapped me is the first honest one I've ever had in my life. I'm not grateful for what happened. I'm not stupid. But I can't be angry about it anymore. Who would I be without it?

I shiver at the thought, and Dario sees me.

"Let's get you where it's warm," he says. "Before you call me a snort."

CHAPTER 34

SARAH

DARIO HUSTLES ME BACK DOWN THE ELEVATOR AND INTO THE CAR, where he turns the heaters on full blast.

"I'm fine," I say, turning the heater down.

At a red light, he touches the top of my ear.

"Yeah... still cold." He turns the heat back up, and though I'm pretty sure I won't get frostbite, I'll take human kindness where I can get it. "What do you want to eat?"

"That!" I point at a yellow-and-red sign I've seen all over the city.

"Papaya King?" He acts as if he didn't really hear me right.

"Yes!"

"It's not a restaurant, really."

"We'll have time, right?"

He pulls the car into a space by a fire hydrant. "Yes, we will."

WE EAT in the front seat of the illegally parked car, watching people appear from and disappear into the Union Square subway station.

"Last bite," he says, holding out a morsel of sausage wrapped in a squashed bun. "Open up."

He feeds me.

"This is really good," I say between chews. "Also really bad."

"Exactly." He stuffs the wrappings into the paper bag.

"Like you." I take the last of my juice, swirl the ice in the bottom of the Styrofoam cup, and suck the straw until the bottom crackles with disappointment.

The streetlights shade his face enough that when he smirks, I notice a dimple for the first time.

"You don't have to give me that much credit."

His smirk is a promise and a dare. It's a demand and a request.

"How many women have you broken with that smile?"

"One," he says, running his thumb on the thick-stitched seam in the steering wheel. "The rest didn't get close enough to break." He shakes his head and looks far away. "But that one?" He makes an exploding sound and holds his hands out as if he's gripping a quickly expanding balloon. "Like falling on tempered glass."

"I've never fallen on tempered glass."

"Of course." He laughs. "Funny story." He glances out the window in a moment of doubt, then continues anyway. "I was almost eleven. Nico—about nine. And we were done with our father."

"Why done?"

"Forget that part. This is the story. We decided we were

big enough take care of him." He leans close as if telling me a secret he's always wanted to claim. "Every night, our father had a big glass of Pepsi with dinner. There's so much sugar and toxic garbage in there you can't taste three milligrams of Rohypnol."

"What is that?"

"A drug. It knocks you out. I got it from an eighth-grader."

Out the driver's side window, a group of half a dozen skater kids practice flipping their boards underfoot. They are amazing, agile, stubbornly practicing the same thing over and over.

"Got it." A boy lands a trick and pumps his fist. "Go on."

"We gave our mother a little." He holds thumb and finger close together. "So she'd sleep through it. After dinner, Dad dropped on the couch like a bag of rocks. Mom went to bed. Then we put duct tape over his mouth and around his arms and legs and waited for him to wake up."

On the street, someone leans on a car horn, and two more join in as Dario takes a moment gather the story. I'm riveted because I don't know what's next... and yet I do.

"And?" I ask when he takes too long.

"We were kids." He says it as if he's just now realizing the story isn't that funny, but he's committed to telling it.

I nod, releasing him from my judgment.

"We were just going wait until he got up and tell him he had leave and never come back, but he slept so long. He was a big guy, so maybe we overestimated his weight, or maybe we were kids in over our heads. We fell asleep, and a few hours later, we wake up and he's thrashing around the living room. Knocking shit over. He's still groggy, and he's trapped like a cat in a bag, so he can't listen to our stupid ultimatum"—Dario puts on a faux-adult voice—"'Get out or we'll kill you,' and we never thought about how we were getting him *out* of the duct tape. I'm holding up a baseball bat like this, and Nico's got a steak knife. He won't let us near him, and he's twisted it now, so it's tighter and pulling the hair on his arms... It was a fucking mess."

He shakes his head, looking inward at the scene.

"What happened?"

"Anyway, we should get going."

"Dario!" I cry. Though I flinch when I hear myself say his name with such a demanding snip, he doesn't seem bothered. "You have to finish."

He smiles, knowing exactly what he's doing. "You really want to know?"

"Yes. Please."

"Okay, my curious *principessa*," he says, putting his hand in my lap, over mine as if to anchor himself for the rest of the story. "Dad was drugged and taped up. He had no balance. He fell on a glass tabletop. It broke." He repeats the exploding hand gesture. "Our mother woke up. Saw Dad all bloody with twisted duct tape all over him, face all red and pissed off. She was groggy from the Rohypnol, but when she saw me ready to bludgeon my father, she put her hand out, like this..." He holds his hand out to me expectantly, as if asking to hand the bat over. "So, I'm thinking this is all over. We blew it. She's going to take the bat, untie Dad, and everything's going to suck even worse." The faraway look again. Then he clears his throat. "But I'm a kid, and she's my mother, so I give it to her."

Another pause, but the scratch and clack of the flipping

skateboards sets me on edge. I'm not as patient as I was raised to be.

"She says, 'There are three black duffel bags in my closet. Get them. Both of you.' I grab my brother, and sure enough, there were three bags. I don't know how long she was ready to go, but she always intended to take us. We brought them out, and she's standing over him with this bat up, and he's not moving."

He stops and rubs his eyes, smiling as if suppressing a laugh at the absurdity of it, shaking his head as if the next words are too much to bear.

"Did she...?" I let the words drift into silence.

He looks down, his profile a silhouette against the streetlights and movement of Union Square. "He had it coming."

"I believe you."

"Then she used the bat to smash the front doorknob."

"Why?"

"To make it look like a break in. She said, 'Let's go,' and we go. Threw the bat into a dumpster behind the station, and the three of us got on a bus from Philly to New York." He gathers the hot dog and drink containers. "She made a few dozen mistakes, but they never found her."

He gets out. All I can do at this point is sigh as I watch him throw the hot dog and drink containers in the trash, dark coat flapping in the wind as if it's carrying him, eyes darting with dutiful caution and well-earned suspicion on the walk back to the car.

He was raised to be ready to leave and be bold about it. Cut ties and move on.

I was raised to serve and gratify, not to love.

We are a sad couple in a sad world. Sad and doomed. But when he gets back behind the wheel, I can't imagine a life without him.

When we get to the white door of my suite, I expect him to come in, but he stays in the hall.

"Good night," he says.

"Good night." But we linger, and in the quiet between us, I find myself saying, "Thank you for explaining."

"I want you to know." He comes a step closer, laying his hands on my shoulders. "I will not rest until I get my revenge."

"On me?"

"No. Not on you. Never on you. But I'm going to destroy the Colonia. You have to know that."

His words are hard, but his tenderness is a balm, and though I bask in it for a moment, I refuse to trust it. The child who benefitted from his eviction bears no responsibility, but the woman has a lot to answer for. I could have asked my father more questions, been more rebellious when I was told what was what. Instead, I marched through attainments. Constantly getting a pat on the back meant I couldn't see the backs I marched on.

"I should have done better," I repeat. "I can't change that, but I can change what happens next."

I feel something catching inside me, a match striking—ready to burn it all down.

"You are stronger than you know."

The sound of his voice rumbles through my body,

warming my bones. I feel more exposed than when my knees were spread before him. Desire flickers between my legs and in my throat. I'm wet. He is demanding nothing of me, and I'll offer it all the same.

I've been shattered by everything I've learned, desperate for someone to rush into the void where my community's love once filled my heart.

He can have my body. It's already his.

Instead, he draws back.

"It's been a long day," he says. "Do you have everything you need for the night?"

I nod when I mean to say no.

Because I don't have everything I'll need tonight.

I don't have anything I need because he's not coming inside.

"Good." He steps away. The hall seems too short now. Walls will be between us before I have the chance to say anything.

"Dario," I say. He stops, ready to listen. "You don't have to go."

I open my mouth before I know what's coming out of it, and he sucks in a breath, closing the gap between up from three steps, two feet, six inches, a sliver of space away—wide enough for electrically activated air—then that snaps closed under the force of his velocity. Then his mouth, his tongue, his hands are seeking me in a kiss I can feel from my lips to the flow between my legs.

His hands cup my jaw like a grail. He's passionate and starving for this kiss but generous. Responsive. Lavish with his attention, as if he's the richest man in the world and he's spending every dime on devotion.

My body is aroused, but something else is happening. A curious uplift takes hold of me, and though I feel as though I'm about to hit the ceiling, I forget how to stand.

With a gasp, he pulls away, and we breathe together, like one person with one thought on their mind.

"Come inside," I say. "Whatever happens tomorrow or the next day, just come inside now."

"I can't anymore." He kisses me between every word. "I can't hurt you. I won't."

"Yes, you can," I say, melting under his attention. "And you will."

He sighs and submits to me.

CHAPTER 35

SARAH

WE WALK, KISS, UNDRESS AT THE SAME TIME, HIS LIPS SINGEING mine. My fist tightens on his coat and pushes away the shoulders. It falls, and we kiss as he unzips my coat and wrestles me out of it.

I clutch his shirt, riding the force of him like a wave. He pulls my skirt up with one hand, gathering the fabric in his fist as he slips a hand between my legs and grazes his fingers searchingly against the damp crotch of my underwear.

"Oh, princess," he says. "Have you been this wet for me this whole time?"

"Yes."

Two fingers press my panties to the side and find my soft core, and it's so intense I hitch my leg over his hip, gasping into the shoulder of his shirt.

"Take me," I say because I can give only what he's willing to take. "Take it all."

With a tender kiss to the bridge of my nose, he pushes me to my knees, and with a touch that's a warning of how

243

I'm going to be handled, he jerks my chin up to look at him. He towers over me and peels off his shirt. He's hard-muscled and taut-skinned, rippling with strength and power, taking in the sight of me on the floor not with the hunger of a starving man, but the appetite of a predator calculating which part of his captured prey to eat first.

"I have already." All business, he unfastens his pants. "When I married you I owned your body. But when I told you my story, I took your soul."

"It's yours." I reach for the bulge stretching his underwear, but he slaps my hands away and gets out of his trousers to take out his dick. The skin is red and tight, throbbing as if it's angry. "Take care of it."

He's above me now, completely naked, fisting his cock like a man ready to bludgeon me with it.

I wait on my knees, vulnerable, giving.

He leans down, scoops me up, and puts me in the wingback chair by the window.

"Stay here." He goes to the kitchen and comes back with a glass of water.

"Thank you." I drink.

"I never saw anything as beautiful as your face when you don't have any doubts."

Finishing the last drop, I take a deep breath.

"I have plenty." I give him the glass and gather my skirt over my knees.

He puts down the glass and leans over me. "About me?"

"Yes."

"You're a very smart woman."

He kisses me, exploring the edges and corners of my mouth, while he pushes my bra and sweater up over my breasts to get to the waistband of the skirt. I lift my bottom so he can slide it off, underpants and all, then he hooks his hands under my knees, spreading them apart and lifting them over the arms of the chair.

Standing with a dick that's already erect, he spins a chair to face mine and sits, casually looking at my disarray. My bra squeezes the tops of my breasts just above hard nipples, and my wide-open legs expose my soft, wet need. I'm swollen and wet for him already, and he can see it.

"Open your cunt," he says. "Show me how wet you are."

My body responds to this utter debasement by turning hot enough to boil blood and melt bone. I lay my hands on my labia and spread them apart.

"I'll keep you. But I may still hurt you."

"I know."

Dario bends my legs up and farther apart. "Hands behind your head." He pulls my lips apart, examining what they hide. "I don't think you really understand."

Either he's underestimating me, or I'm underestimating him. Fine. But I can't fear getting hurt while he inspects me with efficient, almost sexless intensity, peeling back layers to expose my throbbing clitoris and wet opening, pushing my hips off the cushion to spread my ass apart for his scrutiny.

He runs the backs of his fingers along my clit. "I'm going to hurt you the way I hurt everything I've taken."

He slaps between my legs. I yip and arch, and even though I moan in pleasure, my legs close from the pain.

"Again," I whisper, spreading my knees apart. "Please."

Leaning back, he takes stock of my open legs, the dripping wetness between them. He gathers moisture from my opening to draw his touch up and circle my clit. I'm close to orgasm. Too close to warn him when he gets on his knees and gives the quickest little lick where I'm sensitive and swollen, sending a shot of fire through me so hard my eyes close and the world goes black in a split second of thoughtless bliss.

"You just came," he says, unsurprised.

"Rule five. I'm sorry."

"Get on the bed."

It's two steps to the bed, but I make it in one.

"You'll be punished for that." He runs his lips between my thighs.

"How?"

He runs his tongue along oversensitive tissue. "With freedom."

"Freedom?"

He sucks on my clit. The discomfort moves aside for the push of pleasure.

"To come when you want." He flicks and fingers, sucks and licks. "Once."

"Now?"

Though he's below me, telling me I can do what I want, when he looks up, he is the one in charge.

"Whenever you want."

He drops his gaze and works on me with his tongue, and his lips, and his hands. I thread my fingers through his hair, pulling him closer, jerking against his face until the heat is unbearable.

"Can I come?" I ask, forgetting anything but the rules.

He doesn't answer. Just sucks harder.

"Please, can I..."

The orgasm expands, breaking the shell of consciousness like tempered glass into a million sparkling blue-white pieces.

He's kissing me. His lips taste like sex.

"You asked permission."

"Does that mean I get another freebie?"

He gets on his knees and edges himself between my legs.

"This cunt?" He holds down my left leg and yanks up my right leg, twisting me to my side, cheek against the mattress, and drives two fingers inside. "It's my toy." He drapes my left leg over his shoulder, straddling the other. "And I break my toys."

"Break it," I squeak, hips twisted and scissored with his. "Please."

The head of his cock is just at my opening.

"You come when I tell you to. Not before." He pushes into me, hard.

I release a sound that's half cry of hurt, half moan of satisfaction.

"Never," he exhales, and I don't know if he's encouraging me or giving himself permission before he drives forward again, stretching me as if it's the first time, but I move into him as he thrusts deeper, until he's pushing against my body's limits, and he stops for a moment.

I know what he needs.

"Yes!" I cry, and again he lets go of a breath.

"So fucking tight." He lunges deep, root to tip, jerking against my clit.

He handles me like a doll he's going to use up and throw away, except he's keeping me. Possessing me. His hands push and pull, grab and twist. The position is uncomfortable and he's careless and rough, angling himself deeper, opening my legs wider so he can peel me raw, down to electricity. So many sensations fight for my attention I'm sure I won't come. I came twice already.

But he wets two fingers with his tongue and puts them on my clit, circling while he's deep inside me.

"The first time I saw this body"—he leans down so close I feel his breath on my face—"I wanted to strip it down. Make it shake." He moves his dick out, then in again, still circling with his finger. "The first time I fucked it, I knew I wasn't letting it go."

"Let me come."

"No." He slams into me twice, grunting, rubbing harder.

"Please."

He puts his fingers in my mouth. I taste the musk of my pussy on two fingers, then three as he shoves them deep as he fucks me. When he takes them out and resumes the circles on my clit, they're slick with enough spit to slide effortlessly.

"You're so close."

"Need to. Please."

"No."

He jerks, core-deep, flicking, circling, pushing the boundaries of my resistance without giving me permission until I can't take it another second.

My heart is obedient, but my body wicked and brazen, submitting to a howling orgasm that shakes against him.

He doesn't acknowledge it but keeps stroking me.

"Take it until I tell you to stop," he grunts, pure animal.

The orgasm's pleasure turns in on itself, twisting and

shuddering, inside out. Neither pain nor pleasure, but both. The agonizing bliss is too much.

"Now, you can come," he says through his teeth, releasing into me.

Like an obedient Colonia wife, I come again.

CHAPTER 36

SARAH

HE PICKS ME UP AND BRINGS ME TO THE BATHROOM, A THIN-skinned sack of used up flesh without a single bone to fight gravity. More horizontal than the horizon. Parts drop off me and fall into the cracks between the floorboards and the molecules of concrete, dropping limp into the center of the earth, where it's so loud you can hear a pin drop.

He lays me on the little love seat in the powder room that's adjacent to the sinks and bath, and my body drapes over the tufting like a yard and a half of fine silk.

I'm not convinced I'm completely conscious.

To test it, I count my orgasms and say a word. "Four."

"I'm not a stingy husband." He turns on the heater. "That's the least you should expect."

"It's too much." My head is on the arm of the sofa, and one foot's on the little rug under it. A bar of light streams through a small window, but the room is otherwise dusk dark.

"Most women search their whole lives for a man who

gives a shit if they come." He kneels on the floor next to me. "You got lucky on the first try."

"I don't feel lucky."

"No? How do you feel?" He shifts my legs so he can inspect the soreness between them. I relax, letting him assess the change in my body.

"Wiped out."

"I knew I'd be too rough with you."

"You weren't," I say, but when he raises an eyebrow at me, I laugh. "Okay. You were."

"I wanted to eat you alive." He kisses inside my thigh, close to where he broke me but not where it hurts.

When he stands over me, I feel the heaviness of his gaze on my throat, my breasts, the curve of my hips. As I bend to stand, he quickly leans over and tugs at the hem of my sweater. I lift my arms so he can take it off.

I catch my reflection in the mirror. I've been through the wringer. I am small and unfinished.

"I'll clean myself up and come back out."

He stands still, feet spread, dick wet and half-hard.

"Go on," I add a little more forcefully. "I'll be done in a minute,"

He leaves, but only long enough for me to start a bath. When he returns, he's as still as a painting, holding his fist under the cone of light from the window. It casts shadows on his tight jaw, his dark, arched eyebrows, and the careless precision of the hair dropping over his tightly knotted forehead.

He opens his fingers. The six-pointed ring he gave me at our wedding rests in his palm.

"There it is," I say.

"It's garbage." He tosses it on the vanity, then flips open the cabinet and takes out a few tubes. A jar. He shakes a bottle to see what's left in it. "I take good care of the things I value."

The vast array of half-filled choices takes on new meaning. The list of women sent to a paradise.

You should see the beautiful girls here.

He saved me.

"Dario," I say.

"Hm?"

"How many women have you 'valued' in this bathroom?"

He looks at me past the purple tube he's reading like a student presented with a math question on an English test.

The products are an admission that he's had other women here, in this apartment, with him. I'm jealous, and I hate it, but I hold my breath for him to say none. Zero women. I'll only exhale the moment I believe it.

"This isn't my bathroom." He snaps the cabinet closed, picks up a bottle, and unscrews it, sniffing it before dumping a bunch into the steaming water. "Now get in."

I obey, sliding into the hot, balmed bath, then he joins me, displacing enough water to send waves splashing over the edge.

"This is... was... a way station for other women, all of whom I value." He dunks a fresh washcloth, wrings it, and runs it over my body with powerful and efficient generosity. "But I never fucked any of them. Not one."

When Oria told me he was capable of kindness, I didn't believe her. A part of me still doesn't.

"Was Oria one of those women?"

252

He wrings out the cloth. "Close your eyes."

I do it and soon feel the warm fabric on my eyelids.

"She says you saved her."

I can't see him, but I know the position of his body from the way one hand presses on my eyes and one on the back of my neck. He's firm but tender. Commanding and caring. Taking charge while he kneels before me.

"She saved herself," he says. "We were just ready for her." The cloth comes away, leaving him splendid in his nakedness.

"How many are there like Oria?" I ask.

"Hundreds."

"I mean, how many passed through here?"

"Twenty-seven over twelve years."

"And my mother?"

"One of the first."

"Was she the only Colonia?" I fully expect him to say yes because no one just leaves. There's no reason to. We take care of our own. And Oria, the young sex slave, couldn't have been—

"They are all Colonia."

My mind goes as silent as a stone room with air as still as death and a single denial echoing off the walls.

No.

"That can't be." I try to sound casual instead of panicked that my entire life is buttressed up by a rotting arch of deception that I mistook for love.

"It is the truth."

That has to be a lie. Everything he says is false.

"Even Oria?" I ask again.

"Yes."

From the beginning, there was something familiar about her. Not that I ever knew her personally, but her tone, her movements, her way of softening away any insult and anger.

Colonia knows Colonia, even when we don't.

"Dario," I whisper, "I don't know what's happening. What Oria described, it's not us. It's not what we do."

"It's exactly what you do."

I sit up straight in the tub, about to deny it all, but I'm disarmed by his expression.

He pities me.

"Get out," I roar. "I'll finish myself. Just *get out*."

He obeys but stands above me like an angry god. He's about to roar back—tell me I'm not the one giving orders around here. Fuck me and hurt me until I'm out of resistance.

But he blinks. I blink. And as I'm about to apologize, he walks out, closing the door behind him.

In the silence he leaves, I think I may have gone too far.

I'm sheltered and limited, more inexperienced and ignorant than I ever thought possible. I've never been out of the city, much less the country.

How much of my own life have I missed?

Who have I missed?

In a towel, I burst into the bedroom. He's already dressed, sliding his thumb over his phone.

"Wanda Travera. She died last year, but someone said they saw her—"

"She's one of mine." He puts the phone in his pocket.

"I went to the funeral," I object.

"Closed casket, I assume?"

"So?"

"So" means "yes," and he knows it.

"So" means Wanda Travera suddenly got sick and died behind closed doors, and Lili didn't see her mother's body for no other reason than that Louis Travera decided he didn't want the lid open.

My father said my mother's face was in no condition for an open casket.

I was grateful.

Lili hadn't been surprised. She said her mother must have died having one of her ugly days. Those always followed Mr. Travera giving her a correction. Lili said her mother died of defiance. She believed that the way I believed my mother had been too badly beaten by an outsider to see.

"You're saying she left," I confirm. "She 'rescued herself,' and not only did her husband tell everyone she died, but our entire system was in on it. Our doctors. Our mortician. Our leaders—"

My father.

No. My point would render the tangent moot.

"—all buried an empty casket."

I'd chosen to believe the foolishness of a woman's body spontaneously being ugly the days following her husband's anger, and as sheltered as I am... that my mother strolled out unaccompanied long enough to be attacked... and now I continue to defend the same foolishness out of habit.

"Yes," he says.

"Sure." I open my top drawer and pull out clothes, barely looking at them. "Whatever you say."

"What did you think happened to your mother?"

Turning to the shadowed ceiling, I bark a laugh at

myself because the question cuts through the facile choices of my belief system, and I'm forced to say what I always assumed but never dared to say to myself.

How was my mother out without an escort?

There are things I didn't dare think but knew and things I thought but never knew.

This one thing—this nonverbal seed—now has just enough water to germinate.

"I thought he killed her."

Dario says nothing. He knows I mean my father.

I put on underwear, and everything is fine. It's fine when I put the T-shirt over my head. I've lived my entire life in a windowless box, and it's just fine.

"There's something you're not asking about," he says.

"It's fine."

"Your mother—"

"I said it's fine!" I shove my feet into a pair of soft pants but leave them halfway up my thighs to put my hands over my face as I recite, "'*Dearest Dario—You should see the beautiful girls here... and they'd love to see you. All my love—Willa.*'"

"The postcard."

"Is she there?"

"No. But we got her out."

I'm still hunched, but I get my face out of my hands. "How?"

"I can't say. I won't. It's too risky for everyone. She did stay here. But she ran before we could send her to the island."

I sit on the bed and wedge my hands between my knees. She was right here, in this suite. I've lived here for how long and didn't even know it?

Dario sits next to me. "Do you want to go back? Leave here?"

If this is a choice I'm being given—between cold and warmth, danger and safety, enslavement and freedom—it's impossible. I'm too scared of both. Grandma said women make choices out of cowardice, which is why men make all the decisions.

"No." I take my hands away.

I want to believe the slight smile he suppresses means he's pleased with my answer, but I fear I'm misreading everything about him. I wasn't taught to make big decisions about my life. That was done for me. All I've been prepared to do is obey and trust.

"You'll be safe there," he says like a priest promising salvation during a crisis of faith. "The Colonia won't ever stop looking for me and, by extension, you. So, even if you're ever safe here, you'll never be free."

He's not clarifying my choices, and he knows it. He's asking if I'd choose to stay with him even when I'm not in the middle of having sex with him.

And maybe he's rethinking the promises he made in the heat of passion.

I take too long to answer. He gets up and opens the closet, reaching to a high shelf for a suitcase. He drops it on the bed and snaps it open.

He's changed his mind.

I have to make a conscious decision to breathe.

Hold it.

Don't cry.

Exhale.

Don't beg.

"Pack up what you have," he says. "I'll buy you whatever else."

Breathe. Hold it. Exhale.

"I—" It comes out as *uh* and is interrupted by two quick hitches before I can finish.

I don't want to go.

Dario shakes his head and opens my dresser.

"If there's a product or whatever you want from the bathroom, grab it." He lifts out my three pairs of pants. "I'll get you your own tom—"

Seeing me, he stops himself, and in the comfort of his gaze, I have the courage to finish my sentence.

"I don't want to go."

"Sarah." He drops the clothes into the suitcase.

"I won't." I clench my fists. "You can't make me. If my mother ran away, I can too!"

He picks up my left hand and rubs the fist loose before locking it into his right. The scars on the lowest parts of our fingers match up like puzzle pieces.

"You're staying with me."

"I am?" I glance at the bed. That's definitely a suitcase.

I have to stop to swallow a sticky wad of disappointment. He takes me by the shoulders, and I almost break into sobs, convinced he's about to tell me I'm going to love the beaches and blue skies of paradise.

"Yes. Down the hall."

"And then?"

Then I'll be driven to the airport and—

"You're going to live with me."

"Down the hall..." I almost collapse with relief. "With you."

"With me." He gently pulls me onto the mattress, where I curl up against his chest.

I've been lied to, abandoned, and broken. I've been shunned and stolen. I've spent too much of my life being told how to react to a man's body. I was never told to listen to his heartbeat or warned how the comfort of his embrace would firmly pull the threads of doubt until it unraveled completely, or that the unraveling would reveal such refuge underneath.

CHAPTER 37

DARIO

THE DRAWINGS ARE PUT AWAY, BUT I GET THEM OUT AND SIFT through them in the dark. Mostly, they're renderings of things around my apartment and her suite. The clock on the desk, a pen, two vases with complementary shapes. They're simple drawings of simple things, but they have their own glow. An unfinished self-portrait has joined the still lifes. The lines are razor-thin with shading in only the darkest areas—the corners of her mouth and eyes, her pupils, one eyebrow. She looks as if she's walking through a mist, moments from being fully visible. It's perfect. I don't want her to finish it.

It's been five days since Sarah moved in with me. Five days of her body and artful attention to my every need. Five nights exploring her body, going blind with lust, and getting up in the dark hours of the morning asking myself what the fuck I think I'm doing.

What am I doing?

She crowds my mind. Her sheltered past. Our shared present. What I can do for her, with her, to her.

Down below, the city moves at its usual pace. Brake lights crawl into the Lincoln Tunnel like a red-spotted snake eating its tail. In the bedroom, Sarah is sleeping softly, naked, breathing deeply in sleep for another few hours.

When she wakes, I'll be gone, as always, and I'll be back at night, after my work is done.

I've never claimed to be a decent person. I do good for my own good. Fucking over the Colonia by rescuing its beaten, trapped women isn't some noble thing I do for its own sake. That's bullshit. I do it because it hurts Peter Colonia, who killed my mother.

The fact that every time we get a woman out, some Colonia guy loses his mind feeds my need for revenge.

As the days go by, it's clear I'm keeping Sarah. She's not going to St. Eustatius.

At first, I would have said I was keeping Sarah to spite Peter and his whole cult. Make them eat their own shit daily. Imagine her father trying to maintain the Agosti alliance, chewing the inside of his face over losing his daughter so publicly. Sometimes, I even toy with the idea that he loves her and worries about her being in bed with me—criminal savage that I am.

But that's a lie I can't tell myself anymore.

Up until a few days ago, revenge woke me in the morning and sang me to sleep at night. I constantly worked toward it. Accumulated money and property to execute it, lived for the next plan, the next attack, the next win.

Then there was StuyTown. How Sarah looked on the roof overlooking the East River, the sun's last rays high-

261

lighting her silhouette, graceful even under the bulky coat. Her sly smile when she teased me. The expression on her face when she talked about the ferry haunts me.

I don't want some half stranger in my bed ever again. I want Sarah—her helpless gasps when she's surprised, her grunt when pain and pleasure mix, and her wholehearted submission. I want her prodding questions, her prideful walk, her gentle naïveté. She comes undone every time I touch her, but somehow she puts herself back together again.

"Do you want coffee?" Her voice is soft with sleep. She leans in the doorway between my bedroom and living room, hugging a thick white robe around her.

"It's early. You should go back to sleep."

But she's already in the dark kitchen, taking care of my needs. I didn't know I had any until I stole her.

"We're low," she says, shaking a jar containing the three remaining coffee pods.

"I'll send someone." I brush a stray curl from her cheek. The hair is tucked away, but something is still wrong. "Talk to me."

"When I came here, this kitchen was the most barren thing I've ever seen in my life. You had an expired can of beans and this..." She waves in disdain. "Quick Lick noodle cup."

"It's delicious."

"Nothing in the refrigerator but old condiments in the door." She opens the silverware drawer to get a spoon from the stock of plastic cutlery, a screwdriver, a tape measure, and a box of tacks, all jumbled together like a game of Jack Straws. "You live like you're leaving."

I slide behind her, a hand on each side, leaning on the counter. She's trapped.

"I'm not leaving," I murmur against the back of her neck.

"I guess my point is that I need to."

The boner against her ass shrinks to fucking nothing. She's not leaving. Never.

"I don't know whether to spank you once for that..." I kiss the back of her neck. "Or spank you twice."

"Is that a threat?"

"Depends on which one I choose."

Within the cage of my arms, she turns around.

"I made lists, and you sent people out with them, but I'm used to going shopping with a group of women, not sitting here and waiting. And you're going to tell me to go with Oria and Dafne. But Dario... if this is my life now... I want to live it."

Her words are a slap in the face. A wake-up call. She has no idea what her freedom will cost me.

CHAPTER 38

SARAH

HIS APARTMENT INCLUDES THE DINING ROOM WHERE HE SPANKED and fucked me. The rest looks more lived-in and warmer than the Valued Woman Suite, but the truth of the matter revealed itself in the dusty pantry. The refrigerator door was empty. An egg carton was occupied by two tenants, and judging from the date on the side, the rent was already three days late.

"I want to live it," I say.

His face falls, and his lips tighten. "You want your freedom."

"I want to go grocery shopping."

"I'll send you out with Connor."

"No Connor. Just me. Whenever I want."

"Have you ever gone grocery shopping by yourself?"

The answer is no, and he knows it.

"Please." I lay my hands on his chest. The palms are dry against the fabric. "I have to find a way to exist."

"You are my responsibility. You are my property."

"And you value me," I say. "I know."

"More than value. I adore you. I honor you. I treasure you." His hands slide into the robe, grabbing both pebbles at the apex of my breasts. "And I want you." He pulls off my robe, leaving me naked, and kicks apart my feet.

"Take me, then." I bend one leg around his waist. "But let me go."

He's made of fire, a cruel god of destruction, and I am his willing sacrifice, bent backward over a granite altar.

"Oh, Sarah." He releases his cock and guides it to where I'm wet and waiting. "You're such a beautiful problem."

He pushes into my pussy, so big I'm stretched all over again. I'll never get used to his ruthlessly slow, deep strokes, his dick so thick, so deep in me that all I can do is breathe and take it.

"You're going to go downstairs," he growls, taking me by the hips to jerk me into him. "Walk to Eighth Avenue. Get me what the fuck I ask for, come back here, and cook it."

"You'll tell me where to—" The rest is lost in a gasp.

"And you'll go there and no place else."

"Yes."

"Not a step off the route," he says, and I realize he's saying that because I'll be alone. I can escape into the crowd or make a wrong turn and get lost.

A twinge of terror threads itself through the comforts of sex.

Before I can say no, that I've changed my mind and can't go alone because I've never been out by myself, his thrusts get shorter, sharper, jolting my hips, and I'm a doll again. I don't bleed or feel. I am made of hollow plastic and rubber, filled with the hard tar of desire. Dario is the fire that heats it to a boiling, sticky pitch, melting my shell from the inside out.

"You're going to come." Dario grabs my ass hard enough to get a gasp. "Then you're going to go out with a sore cunt full of my come."

When he reaches down to rub my clit, the pliable shell thins under the pressure inside. It'll be breached soon, and I'll spill into a sticky puddle onto the floor.

"I'm close," I gasp, shaking and pinned in place as Dario fucks me and rubs me. All I can do is grunt and lose myself to the heat, boiling away the shell of a membrane from the inside.

"Come for me."

His command is almost a whisper, but it's all I need to let go, pulse around him, tugging him in as deep as I can get him, the thick head of his dick slicing me open to release pitch-dark bliss. He spills open with me, his hips stuttering, his control only wavering in this unbound, otherworldly, fleeting death.

He gathers me in his arms, chest expanding and contracting against mine. We fold into each other like a riddle and its answer. I don't know how I'm standing until he straightens himself and I realize he was holding me up the entire time.

CHAPTER 39

DARIO

Sarah left nervous.

I told my guys to stand down and let her walk out. She's not a prisoner. She's my wife, and she's going to the bodega for Quick Lick ramen, which I don't even like that much, but which she's going to prepare naked, and once the noodles cool off, I'm going to suck them off her tits.

A wedge of Eighth Avenue is visible from the bedroom window. When she left, I watched it for a sign of her. Now, what feels like seven hours later but is actually twelve minutes, I'm watching for the return pass.

What if I run away?

She asked me as I handed her a ten-dollar bill, as if running were a real possibility and she needed to know what I'd do.

I replied as if it were a possibility because I know what I'd do, but what would she do?

Where would you go?

She folded the money and stood there with the rectangle

in her palm as if she didn't know where to put it. I plucked it
from her hand and slid it into her front pocket.

I'd look for my mother. I don't know where.

Gennaro offered to go with her, but she refused before I
could rethink my decision to let her go alone two blocks.

I've been too confident. Sure she won't leave. Can't.
She's mine. My wife. Her whole life's been built around me.

I own her.

*You'd start at the Department of Health on Court Street
where they keep the death certificates.*

It wouldn't be that simple. Like all of them, Mary
Ballardo-Colonia didn't have a birth certificate. After she
escaped, she may have taken a different name. She might
have gotten remarried. She probably died of exposure in any
of the winters between her exile and today. But my wife
wouldn't have it.

You think she's dead? Her eyes narrowed, daring me.

I let her think her mother could be alive, then I told her
where to go, how to buy a thing, and sent her around the
corner with a promise that I wouldn't follow.

Now I'm watching out the window, waiting for her to
cross the street.

Still, forty seconds later, she hasn't walked into that pie-
slice-shaped bit of sidewalk, and the only reason I haven't
bounded down of stairs yet is that I lied and sent Connor
behind her.

The phone rings, and before I even see the screen, my
growing panic knows it's him.

"Connor," I bark.

"Hey, I—"

"Where is she?"

"I can't—"

His voice drops into meaningless syllables.

"Conn—!"

"—other side of—"

"Shit! Fuck!"

"—there's a—"

She's gone.

Taken or escaped.

Out of my hands.

I run out, taking the stairs three at a time because the elevator's too slow and it's crystal clear how fucking stupid I am. The massive risk. Not that she was out of my sight. Not even that she's borderline nonfunctional.

No.

By the eighth floor, I know I've assessed those risks and come out on the right side. The danger I neglected is the one that's eating my guts now.

The Colonia. Her father. Sergio Agosti. They want her, and yes, her location is hidden behind walls of complications and dead ends, and yes, I'm a needle and the city is a twenty-three-square-mile haystack.

But also, yes... they have enough power to buy a lucky break. That's all it could take to find us. They don't have to storm past security or blow shit up.

They have to stand outside and wait for her to come out.

Which they must have done.

Leveraging myself on the railings to jump the corners, I'm convinced this is exactly what's happening.

My feet barely touch the landings.

7TH FLOOR

I'm convinced she walked out with ten dollars in her

pocket and a hand-drawn map of the bodega with a list of instructions titled "How to Buy Shit."

A Colonia stooge spotted her.

5TH FLOOR

Stooge called Cult HQ. She's out. She's alone. She's heading to Tenth.

The Colonia car swings around and pulls up to the curb.

4TH FLOOR

A woman she trusts, probably her grandmother, gets out of the car, says hello.

3RD FLOOR

Tells some bullshit lie or recites some code words and Sarah's brain triggers all the safety and happiness she ever had in her life.

LOBBY

She gets in the car, and she's gone.

End of story. This is how it goes down in my mind, but it's not the end of the story. I will not live without her. I will not let them take her.

I will find her.

Gone. Gone.

I leap into the lobby and slip on the marble floor, sweating.

Gone.

Run for the exit to 47th Street.

She's gone.

I will raze the earth.

Burn the city.

Spill the blood of anyone between us.

"Dario!"

Her voice echoes against the stone floors and high ceiling, but she's nowhere. Gone.

It was definitely her, but where is she?

Gone.

Connor comes in off the street.

Alone. Not with her. I imagined it.

It couldn't have been Connor calling me by my first name. It's her. I know it, but I don't see her, and I've been wrong before.

"Hey."

Her voice again. I spin and find Sarah, my wife... my beautiful wife... standing three feet away with pink cheeks and brown hair falling out of her braid, holding out a white plastic bag.

"I did it!"

"You did!"

I say it in her ear because I've already gathered her up in my arms, lifting her off the floor. When I kiss her, it's not on her mouth, but on her neck, where thin skin covers her artery, and her pulse jumps against my lips.

She's never leaving me again.

CHAPTER 40

SARAH

In the elevator, I try to hit the top floor, where we live, but it won't light up.

Dario uses a card to make it go, but he also kisses me.

And kisses me.

He's left Connor in the lobby so he can kiss me more than he's ever kissed me before, but this time is different.

He's different. He's not simply proud of me for making it to the store and back.

There's an unknownness about his touch; a learning, a teaching, to his lips; and a listening and feeling in the darting, curious explorations of his tongue.

"Dario," I say, pushing him gently. "What happened?"

"You're back." He runs his mouth over the length of my neck, caressing the other side with his thumb, keeping my chin pointed up.

"Where did you think I went?"

The elevator dings, and the doors open. He pulls me out and pushes me against the hallway wall, holding my hands over my head. The plastic bag dangles from my thumb as he kisses my face and neck.

"Please," I say. "Just tell me."

"If they take you, I will find you."

"Who?"

"I will dismantle the city."

"My father?"

He doesn't stop to confirm but lets my arms go so he can take my jaw in his hands. "I will reduce them to dust. I am your husband, and they will not have you to sell or use ever, ever again."

"Dario..." I put my hands on his chest, sorry to tear the fabric of his sweet delusion. "They don't want me."

"They don't want you the way I do. But trust me... they want you where they can control you. I don't know how they're going to try to get you, I don't know when, but if they come for you, I'm ready for them."

He locks me in a stare hot with passion and intention.

I believe him, but he's wrong. They let my mother go. Without a word or whisper, they let go of the twenty-seven girls he sent to an island. I'm not special. We're all worth the same if we're all worthless.

Agreeing that he's right means leaving the nationless in-between for a place darker than I can bear. I'd have to stop asking where I belong because it wouldn't matter. I'd be no one.

"I believe you'd do it," I say. "But I was talking to the guy at the store about these noodles."

His laughter cools his intensity. "Really?"

"He said if you add an egg, it's not bad, and the expired ones you have are probably still okay."

"You asked him?"

"He knows his product."

"Of course he does."

He leans in to kiss me, but the elevator arrives and Dario's watch goes off. *One-two, one-two-three. One-*

He shuts it off.

"I'll boil the water," I say, holding up the plastic bag. I don't need to see the watch to know it's NL.

"Thank you." Dario kisses my cheek before running his thumb across it. "I'm going to show you the entire world."

He goes to the business end of the hall, and I open the metal door to his apartment with a thumbprint.

"Sarah," Dario calls.

"Yes?"

"Have you ever been on the subway?" he asks.

"No."

"After lunch, then."

"Okay."

"Together. You and me."

Dario Lucari, my abductor, my husband, and now my teacher, disappears behind the door.

CHAPTER 41

DARIO

THE SMALL SCREEN'S BLANK. NO NICO.

As the minutes tick by—ten so far—the tension coming off Oria is growing into its own energy source.

These meetings with my brother are sacred... at least until now, interrupted by both Nico's absence and the knocking at the door.

"You should get it," Oria whispers.

"Five minutes!" I shout.

The knocking stops.

The pull to find out what they want is almost as strong as the pull to punch Nico in the face. I need this meeting done. I have plans to suck noodles off my wife's body.

"Something happened," she replies. "Waiting's going to make it worse."

"He overslept," I say.

"He's never overslept in his life," Oria says in a voice that's four sizes smaller than the one I'm used to. The voice she was taught to use with men. The one I first heard when

275

she was brought in and I knew destroying the Colonia could be for more than my own gratification. She's here because we hate the same people and we love the same man.

"Maybe," I say, respecting her with the truth of my doubts instead of the gloss of my hopes. "I know you want him to come home. I do too. But if they find Sarah and Nico doesn't have his head right up their asses like he does now, we won't know until it's too late to move."

"So where is he?" She points at the screen where Nico's face is supposed to be.

"Assuming either of us should know is a waste of time," I growl at her because I'm worried too, and she's using that to get what she wants.

I'm saved from an escalation by the resumption of door knocking.

"Fuck this." I jolt up and find Oliver on the other side "What?"

"Tamara's tracking the scanners," he says. "There's been an uptick in SWAT team calls. Like, a big uptick. Lexington and 21st. Seventy-sixth and Fifth. CP West."

Some of the most expensive real estate in the world. Something is very wrong here.

"It's not NYPD. It's the sheriff's."

That explains the urgency. The NYPD goes after crime and criminals, but the NYSD is a civil law enforcement agency headed by the Department of Finance, and the sheriff's department had been infiltrated by Colonia for decades.

"All the buildings have one thing in common," Oliver continues. "They all have a greenhouse on the roof."

CHAPTER 42

SARAH

THE KNOCK ON THE DOOR IS BRASH AND DEMANDING, SO I ASSUME it's Dario. But when I open it, Oria brushes by me, walking right in. I close the door, about to ask her what she wants before I explain that Dario is coming in a minute, but she doesn't stop her stride long enough to listen.

I shut off the burner and find her in the dressing room that leads to the bedroom closet.

"What are you doing?"

She reaches onto a high shelf, pulls down an empty suit-case, and flings it onto the bench under the mirror.

"Pack." She snaps open the case, leaving it spread like a hungry mouth.

"What? Why?"

She seemed so meek and reserved when I met her, but now she's full of aggression, slapping open the pocket door to the closet. His suits are on either side, with racks of shoes and drawers underneath.

"Because you're fucking everything up." She walks to the

back of the closet. "You're fucking him up. You being here is hurting him, and you have to go. Now."

She opens a drawer, but it's full of my husband's things, so she slaps it closed and moves to the next. Still his. *Slap.*

"You're going to St. Eustatius."

"Did Dario say that?" I ask.

"There are people there who can help you, okay?" She whirlwinds through the drawers, making sure I haven't left a single button behind. "I swear it's nice. Away from everything."

"But he said—"

—he wanted noodles.

"You'll love it," she interrupts, then pulls a folded-up envelope from her back pocket. "It's not about what you want anymore. It's about what's best for everyone." She drops it on top of the clothes in the suitcase. "Passport and first-class tickets. He bought them the day before your wedding. The first wedding. To the Prince of Nothing. Sergio. Open-ended tickets. Just show up and they'll get you on a flight. Easy."

"I'm making him lunch."

"You made him a target, and you're going to get someone I love killed. Okay? Just..." She looks at me for the first time since she came in, and I have no idea what she sees, but it shuts her mouth long enough for me to finish a thought.

"He said I wasn't going."

I'm not even convincing myself that I have the last word, or that what he thinks is best even matters. Or that I see inside his heart at all.

"You know how they'd always say the Colonia was your

family but more?" Oria asks.

"Yes?" I say, incredulous that she could be bringing this up now of all times.

"You obeyed for *everyone*'s good." She zips up the interior pockets of the suitcase. "You married who they said and followed the rules because we were different. We had a responsibility to something bigger than ourselves. Which they used to brainwash us, but that doesn't mean it's not true." She zips the case closed. "It is true, and the best thing for everyone you care about"—she heaves it onto the floor and snaps up the telescoping handle—"is for you to leave."

"What did Dario say?"

"You don't belong here."

"Did he say that? Or do you say that?" Outside, sirens blare as if they know my question is an emergency.

"That doesn't matter if it's true."

Since when does Dario's word not matter? Is he in charge or not? The hierarchy no longer functions. The chain of command is breaking down right before my eyes.

Now, I am left with only one authority.

Myself.

I hold my head high as I stride through my husband's apartment. Down the hall toward the double doors. Oria follows.

"Stop it!" she hisses.

I turn on her. "I don't know what happened to you, but you're not in charge here. You don't make decisions about my life. Dario..." I thrust my arm toward the double doors. "He doesn't either. It's me. I decide where I go and who I go there with. Me. I am free, Oria. I'm not a child, and I'm not anyone's prisoner."

The elevator dings and opens.

"We're all prisoners to something, Sarah."

A woman I've never seen before comes out of the elevator. She's a few years older than I am, with dark bronze skin, a hundred thin, black braids with beads on the ends, and a radiant, feminine beauty that breaks the dullness of the hall.

"Hello," she says with a smile, looking me up and down.

She must be a tenant or a guest who got off on the wrong floor, except you need a key card to get up here and she has one right in her hand.

Then she makes eye contact with Oria. "Hey, you!"

They embrace, rocking back and forth. My palms sweat. I rub them on my pants.

"Thank you for coming," Oria says as they pull away from each other but hold hands.

"I'm sorry it took so long, but you know how it is." She turns to me. "You must be Sarah."

Her hand hovers between us. I'm supposed to shake it, but my palms are wet again.

"My name's Willa," she says, dropping the offer of a handshake.

Dearest Dario—

"Willa's here to take you," Oria says.

You should see the beautiful girls here... and they'd love to see you.

"No." I get out that single word before one of the double doors slaps open.

Dario lunges into the hall like a man expecting to run across it without encountering an obstacle. He stops short. Freezes, eyes darting from Willa to me, then back again.

The way he looks at her...

All my love—Willa

"Willa," he says.

"Dario." Her voice is pure honey. "Oria called a bit ago. Said you might need some help, and I just got tired of waiting. I mean, you *know* how impatient—"

"If I wanted you here, I would have sent for you myself."

He's fighting love or rage. Holding back frustration or joy.

Willa shakes her head and turns to me. "Do you need help getting your things together?"

"She's packed," Oria answers.

She's right. I am all packed and ready to go.

"No," Dario barks. "Willa, I'm sorry you came for nothing, but you need to turn the fuck around and go back where you belong."

"But I'm here."

"There's a lot going on. Sarah, go back and—"

"Baby." Willa *tsks* playfully while I turn into a pile of broken eggshells.

"Don't you fucking call me that."

She tilts her head. "Is that any kind of way to talk to your wife?"

My husband goes white as a sheet. I must look even worse because Willa reacts but directs anger at Dario.

"You didn't tell her?" Willa's incredulous. Maybe I

should be too.

"Tell me what?" My voice is weak and cracked. My fists are balled around a river of sweat.

"I cannot believe—" Willa starts.

"What didn't you tell me?" My shout bounces off the walls of the hall.

"Sarah." He points at me, then the metal door leading to his apartment. "You need to go sit down, and I'll take care of this."

"Am I your wife?"

Our eyes are locked together, and someone lost the key.

"Do what I say."

"Yes or no?"

"Just go!" He tries to stare me to the door, but I do not move.

"Am I your wife?" I'm screaming, rooted to the floor. "Yes or no, Dario."

"Jesus," Oria mumbles from the universe outside our gaze.

"Yes or no!"

He breaks the stare. It settles the question of whether or not I'm his wife.

No is a betrayal, and yes is a lie.

Thank you for reading!

THE NEXT BOOK in the series is *MAKE ME*.

For those of you who waited... thank you for your patience. I'm sorry it took so long.

Make Me probably won't take a year, but I've set the release date very far in advance because I'm weird. If everything goes well, give me four months. You might want to preorder now so you don't forget.

Or you can sign up for my mailing list at cdreiss.com and add christine@cdreiss.com to your contacts.

WHO ARE Santino and Violetta DiLustro? And why is she like that?

Find out in the *DiLustro Arrangement*...a complete mafia romance trilogy.

When he forced me to marry him, I cried for love I'd never know. When he locked me away, I cried for the freedom I lost forever. Every other tear I've shed is for my soul, because I'm falling for the devil himself.

Mafia Bride | Mafia King | Mafia Queen

You can start it now with *MAFIA BRIDE!*

KEEP IN TOUCH!

I've got a really cool Facebook group, a Twitter feed that's 78% political rage-outs, and a TikTok that I've been told is hilarious and that I use to feed my Instagram.

If you're not into social media, sign up for my mailing list.

ALSO BY CD REISS

THE DILUSTRO ARRANGEMENT

An epic mafia romance trilogy.

Some girls dream of marrying a prince, but I never imagined I'd be sold to a king.

Mafia Bride | Mafia King | Mafia Queen

THE GAMES DUET

Adam Steinbeck will give his wife a divorce on one condition. She join him in a remote cabin for 30 days, submitting to his sexual dominance.

Marriage Games | Separation Games

THE EDGE SERIES

Rough. Edgy. Sexy enough to melt in your hands.

Rough Edge | On The Edge | Broken Edge | Over the Edge

THE SUBMISSION SERIES

Monica insists she's not submissive. Jonathan Drazen is going to prove otherwise, but he might fall in love doing it.

One Night With Him | One Year With Him | One Life With Him

CPSIA information can be obtained
at www.ICGtesting.com
Printed in the USA
BVHW080114161122
651983BV00017B/576

9 781942 833833